THE WIRRAL KILLINGS

A Snowdonia Murder Mystery

DI Ruth Hunter Crime Thriller No.#20

SIMON MCCLEAVE

STAMFORD
PUBLISHING

THE WIRRAL KILLINGS

By Simon McCleave

A DI Ruth Hunter Crime Thriller
Book 20

No part of this publication may be reproduced, stored, or transmitted in any form or by any means, electronic, mechanical, photocopying, recording, scanning, or otherwise without written permission from the publisher. It is illegal to copy this book, post it to a website, or distribute it by any other means without permission.

Names, characters, businesses, places, events, and incidents are either the products of the author's imagination or used in a purely fictitious manner. Any resemblance to actual persons, living or dead, or actual events is purely coincidental.

First published by Stamford Publishing Ltd in 2024

Copyright © Simon McCleave, 2024
All rights reserved

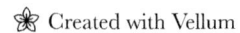

Created with Vellum

BOOKS BY SIMON McCLEAVE

THE DI RUTH HUNTER SERIES

#1. The Snowdonia Killings
#2. The Harlech Beach Killings
#3. The Dee Valley Killings
#4. The Devil's Cliff Killings
#5. The Berwyn River Killings
#6. The White Forest Killings
#7. The Solace Farm Killings
#8. The Menai Bridge Killings
#9. The Conway Harbour Killings
#10. The River Seine Killings
#11. The Lake Vyrnwy Killings
#12. The Chirk Castle Killings
#13. The Portmeirion Killings
#14. The Llandudno Pier Killings
#15. The Denbigh Asylum Killings
#16. The Wrexham Killings
#17. The Colwyn Bay Killings
#18. The Chester Killings
#19. The Llangollen Killings

THE DC RUTH HUNTER MURDER CASE SERIES

#1. Diary of a War Crime
#2. The Razor Gang Murder
#3. An Imitation of Darkness
#4. This is London, SE15

THE ANGLESEY SERIES - DI LAURA HART

#1. The Dark Tide
#2. In Too Deep
#3. Blood on the Shore
#4. The Drowning Isle
#5. Dead in the Water

PSYCHOLOGICAL THRILLER

Last Night at Villa Lucia (Storm Publishing)

Your FREE book is waiting for you now!

Get your FREE copy of the prequel to
the DI Ruth Hunter Series NOW
http://www.simonmccleave.com/vip-email-club
and join my VIP Email Club

Prologue

Heswall, The Wirral, England
August 2021

IT WAS dawn by the time he pulled into the building site. The sun had tinged the early morning sky with pink and orange. As he grabbed his takeaway coffee and got out of the car, he couldn't help but be filled with a sense of excitement as he looked at the housing project in front of him. It was the biggest development of his career. And it was going to net him and his company over £1,000,000 profit by the end of the year. Not bad for a lad from Wrexham with only three GCSEs and an NVQ Level 2 Diploma in Plastering.

He'd already planned what he was going to do with the money. Most of it was going to be ploughed back into another housing development on a plot of land that he'd already bought further up The Wirral in Caldy. This time his company was going to be building 5-bedroom executive homes. In the current market, these houses would sell for a cool £1,500,000 each.

The one luxury that he was going to afford himself was a brand new Range Rover Sport SE. He was still driving around in a Honda CR-V that was nearly ten years old. It was time he started to drive a car that demonstrated the kind of property developer he was.

Then he heard a noise from one of the empty houses.

What the hell was that?

It sounded as if a piece of metal had been dropped. His building team wouldn't be in until 8am.

Resting the coffee carefully on the roof of his car, he wandered across the uneven ground towards where he'd heard the sound.

Then he stopped and listened.

Nothing.

'Hello?' he called out. 'Is someone there?'

He looked over at the huge steel security gates that he'd opened to get on site. They'd increased security as there had been a series of thefts in recent months. Some of the machinery and equipment had been stolen overnight. They were insured, but it was expensive to replace. Even a small JCB digger was £30,000. The police had taken details but they didn't seem particularly interested.

There was another noise.

Footsteps crunching on one of the gravel pathways that had just been constructed.

There's definitely someone here.

Starting to feel uneasy, he wondered if someone had been sleeping rough on the site. If burglars had broken in, why were the gates closed? And surely they would have come in under the cover of darkness, not at first light?

'Hello?' he called again, but this time cautiously. His pulse had quickened.

From out of nowhere, a figure appeared, ran towards him and smashed something metallic against the side of his head before he had time to react.

'Jesus Christ!' he groaned as he saw stars and stumbled backwards.

CRACK!

The figure smashed him again, and then again. He felt a terrible pain across the side of his skull. A piercing pain like nothing he'd felt before.

What the hell is happening?

Trying to get his breath, he felt dizzy. Stumbling. Everything was spinning and out of focus.

His legs went from underneath him as he crumpled to the ground.

He reached out his hand to try and scramble away but the blows had rendered him semi-conscious. He could hardly move or see.

He felt the rough stones and ground under his palms and fingers.

I need to get away, he thought in his terrified stupor. *If I don't get away, they're going to kill me.*

The figure grabbed at his feet and ankles and started to drag him back towards where he'd parked his car.

Digging his fingers into the ground, he tried to stop himself being dragged by clawing at the uneven path underneath him.

It was no use. The attack had taken every ounce of energy and strength from him.

No, no, he said to himself as he tried to struggle. But it was no use.

Hearing a car door open, he became aware that he was now slipping in and out of consciousness.

The figure dragged him up onto his feet for a second.

Trying to get a glimpse of whoever had attacked him, he saw they were wearing a dark hood over their head.

The figure pushed him roughly onto the back seat of his car and slammed the door behind him.

For a fleeting moment, he hoped that the figure had attacked him because he'd stumbled upon them trying to rob the site. They had put him on the back seat of the car to get him out of the way and that would be it.

There were a few seconds of silence.

That's it, he thought. *They'll be gone in a minute.*

Despite the terrible pain in his head, he felt a little moment of relief that the attack was over. He just hoped someone found him soon.

However, he then heard the front passenger door open.

For a moment, he slipped into blackness, his mind trying to make sense of sounds and smells.

What the hell is that?

As he came to again, he knew what he could smell.

Petrol.

The air inside the car was thick with fumes.

Jesus, I can hardly breathe.

Trying desperately to move, he realised it was no use. The attack had left him helpless.

Oh my God! He's going to torch the car, he thought, now full of terror.

He gazed up at the roof of the car as he lay on his back.

Is this it?

The passenger door slammed shut.

Then a horrible sound of crackling and a feeling of heat.

The figure had set fire to the inside of the car.

His eyes and throat began to sting as the car quickly filled with thick black smoke.

Gasping for air, he tried to breathe. He felt like he was drowning.

His head began to spin.

He tried desperately to suck in air. It was no use.

Then everything went black.

Chapter 1

12 hours earlier
Erbistock, Wrexham

DETECTIVE CONSTABLE JIM GARROW of the North Wales Police force had been sitting in the Cross Foxes' beer garden in Erbistock all afternoon, drinking beer. It had a beautiful view across the River Dee and the countryside beyond. He had been due to go to a barbeque at the home of his boss, Detective Inspector Ruth Hunter, just up the road in Bangor-on-Dee, but he was too drunk now. Having popped into the pub for a quick pint on the way, he was now five pints in.

He didn't know what was wrong with him. He felt so completely lost. His actions had resulted in a murder trial being halted and the defendant, Lucy Morgan, being released. Not only did that mean that he was going to face an employment tribunal, but he could also lose his job.

It had been a few months since Lucy Morgan had been found at the Pontcysyllte Aqueduct claiming to have amnesia on the night that her mother, Lynne Morgan, was brutally murdered at her home in Wrexham. Garrow's investigation had eventually discovered that Lucy had slashed her mother's throat after a heated argument and then faked her amnesia to cover her tracks.

However, the major spanner in the works was that Garrow and Lucy had formed a romantic attachment after Lucy had been ruled out as a suspect earlier in the investigation. Although they hadn't slept together, Garrow had been to Lucy's flat. And during the trial, she had claimed they'd had sex. Her defence team had called for a mistrial due to the allegations and the judge had agreed. It was a total disaster.

On top of that, Lucy had started to stalk Garrow, appearing in his garden late at night. The events of the past few days had left him feeling rattled and nervous. He didn't know how any of it was going to turn out.

What Garrow did know is that the overwhelming sense of dread, anxiety and pain seemed to be numbed by alcohol. He was more than aware that he was self-medicating. Anaesthetising himself to block out the distressing thoughts and emotions that seemed to pervade his every waking minute.

As he finished his pint, he gave a sigh. He knew what he'd do. He'd drive via an off-licence on the way home, pick up a bottle of whiskey, and drink the rest of the evening away listening to music. He gave a half smile at the thought of that.

Getting up from the bench seat that he'd been sitting on, he felt a little unsteady on his feet. His head was thick and fuzzy. What if he got pulled over and breathalysed? He gave a snort. He'd never been pulled over in his life so why would that happen tonight?

Walking up the stone steps, he saw an attractive woman

in her 20s coming the other way. They caught each other's eye for just a moment.

She was nice, he thought to himself.

At the back of the pub was another set of stone steps that led to an overflow car park at the top.

The car park was nearly empty as Garrow walked over to his car. The setting sun glimmered orange through the high trees that loomed over him. Then the horrible cawing of a crow from somewhere. He looked up and saw that the branches were littered with crows' nests.

What was the collective noun for crows? A murder? Or was that ravens?

Opening the driver's door, he sat down and shook his head to try and clear it. Then he took a deep breath.

He turned on the ignition. The radio was tuned to BBC Radio 3 and some soft, relaxing classical music was playing.

Vaughan Williams, Garrow thought to himself as he put the car into gear.

Suddenly, a figure appeared from nowhere and stood in front of the car.

It was Lucy Morgan!

Are you bloody joking?

She stared at him with an icy glare.

Rage flowed through him. *Fuck this.*

They locked eyes for a second.

Lucy looked at him as if she was daring him to drive off.

He took a lungful of breath and stamped down on the accelerator.

His car lurched forward at speed, ploughing into Lucy and tossing her high into the air.

Glancing back, he saw her lifeless body lying crumpled in a heap over to the side of the car park.

There was no way he was staying to face the consequences of what he'd just done. He needed to get out of there.

Putting the car back into gear, he screeched out of the car park and sped away into the distance.

Chapter 2

The following morning, DI Ruth Hunter sat back in her padded chair in her office in CID at Llancastell Police Station. Everyone referred to it as the 'nick'. Ruth had assumed that this slang was a London term, but since moving away from the Met she'd found that most places used the word. An old sergeant who Ruth worked with in Battersea in South London had told her that the word 'nick' was actually Australian in origin and dated back to the 18th century. Then her sergeant would make some dubious jokes about all Australians being descended from British criminals, which explained why they were so ill-mannered and foul-mouthed as a nation.

Reaching over for her coffee, Ruth felt a twinge in the back of her leg. It seemed to run all the way down to her feet. It was probably sciatica. She'd had it before. Tight hamstrings. One of the perks of getting old – well older – and doing no exercise. In her head, she was always about to embark on some form of fitness regime. She used to run. In fact, when she first arrived in North Wales she had run every day. She'd managed to whiz through 5k in less than half an hour, which according to articles she read online was a pretty decent time. But she'd let it slip. She promised herself that she would do strength training once a week. Every time she opened an article on her phone, there was something telling her how important it was for women over 50 to do 'resistance training'. To stop muscle 'wastage' and prevent osteoporosis. But then a little voice in her head mocked the idea of going to the gym once or twice a week to lift weights. What if all those muscle-bound 20-something men laughed at her? Then there were plans for a yoga regime. She and Sarah had been attempting to go to a weekly yoga class for over a year. It just never happened. And if she was honest, Ruth was happier sitting in her garden with a cigarette and a large glass of Sauvignon Blanc or Rosé. If that shaved ten years off her life then fuck it. Who wants to get old and wrinkly anyway?

As she gave a long yawn and stretched her arms up, Ruth glanced outside into the main CID office. She saw that 'the troops' were hard at work. The mood was subdued and would be for some time. They had just lost one of their own in the line of duty. Detective Sergeant Dan French. Ruth was still coming to terms with his death. He had been such an integral part of the team and it was a huge loss. It still felt surreal.

The previous evening, Ruth and her deputy, Detective Sergeant Nick Evans, had been up to Dan French's grave. They'd taken some flowers. Ruth had said a few words and shed a few tears.

The visit to the graveyard had reminded her of the last time Llancastell CID had lost an officer. Detective Constable Sian Hockney. Not only had Sian been a brilliant detective, she and Ruth had been in a relationship. Sian had been killed in an armed police operation at Solace Farm on the 12th April 2020. Ruth would never forget that date. Even though they had been split up at the time, she and Sian had been

tentatively back on the road to making their relationship work when Sian had been

killed. That was the cruel irony. And Ruth still felt some guilt about not stopping Sian from going up to Solace Farm that day.

She also felt guilty that she hadn't been up to Sian's grave in a long time. In her mind, she could see Sian's beautiful headstone made from Welsh grey slate and the inscription on it - *Sian Gwyneth Hockney 7.5.1985 – 12.4.2020 'A woman of grace and courage, the song in our hearts.'* Ruth remembered the sound of melodic birdsong – robins, goldfinches, blackbirds and nuthatches – that used to fill the air whenever she'd visited Sian's grave in the months after her death. Ruth would always take a fresh bunch of blue and yellow irises as they were Sian's favourite.

As Ruth sat forward, she could feel tears welling up in her eyes. *Why haven't I been up there in so long?* she wondered. It almost felt that the longer she left it, the harder it was to go back. As if she would owe Sian an apology as to why she hadn't been to see her in so long.

Right, Ruth thought as she wiped the tears from her eyes and hoped it hadn't ruined her makeup, *I'm going up there this weekend. No excuses.*

Chapter 3

Detective Constable Georgina Wild was running late. She felt a little twinge in her stomach. Well, technically it wasn't her stomach, it was her womb. But the thought of having a twinge in her *womb* felt strange and slightly too anatomically correct. It had been several months since Georgie had become pregnant after sleeping with a young journalist, Jake. They had been old friends and had been out together when they were in sixth form. They had met up quite by accident and ended up spending the night together. The tragedy was that he had then been killed in a road traffic accident the following day. Georgie had decided to keep the baby, and everyone at Llancastell CID was doing their best to support her. But if she was honest, there were times in the early hours of the morning when the thought of bringing a baby into the world on her own terrified the life out of her. How on earth was she going to juggle being a single mum with being a detective constable?

Grabbing the car keys from the table in the hallway, Georgie opened the front door and checked her watch. It was 8.23am. It would take her 20 minutes to drive into

Llancastell nick, get parked, grab a coffee and then get to CID just in time for briefing. In the old days – before she was pregnant – Georgie had been one of the first detectives in CID in the morning. She prided herself on sometimes beating her boss, DI Ruth Hunter, in to the office. But the pregnancy was making her tired so she needed every hour of sleep that she could get. And Ruth was more than supportive of that. In fact, she had become a surrogate mother to her in recent months. Georgie had little to do with her own parents who were cold and aloof. They deeply disapproved of her becoming a single mother. But then again, they would, wouldn't they?

Closing and locking the front door, Georgie headed to her car which was parked on the driveway.

A young man in his early 30s came whizzing up the driveway next door on a road bike. He was dressed head to foot in lycra and cycling gear.

Georgie knew that the older couple – Mr and Mrs Bridge – had moved out so they could live nearer to their children down in Welshpool. But Georgie had yet to meet the person, or persons, who had moved in next door a few days earlier. She had just been aware of a removal van and people going in and out of the property. It had been hard to tell who anyone was. She just hoped that whoever moved in were decent people and didn't have mad parties until the early hours.

The young man dismounted from the bike and took off his helmet. His hair was sandy blond and he was very handsome. If she had to guess, Georgie would have had him down as about 30 years old.

Okay, I like the look of him, she thought immediately before checking herself. *He's probably moved in with his girlfriend, AND I'm pregnant. Let's get real here.*

'Morning,' she called over in a cheery voice.

'Oh hi,' the man said, sounding a little out of breath as he got off his bike.

Georgie couldn't work out if he was exhausted from his bike ride or if he was being unfriendly.

Sod it, she thought. *I need to introduce myself.*

'I guess we're neighbours,' she said as she pointed to his house, and then wondered if that was a stupid comment and she was stating the obvious.

'We are,' he replied as he wheeled his bike up the drive and rested it against the front wall of his house. 'I've been meaning to come and say hello. I've just been working nights so I'm a bit all over the place.'

'Right.' Georgie smiled. 'I'm Georgie.'

Okay. He seems friendly enough.

'Georgie,' he said deliberately, as if he was saying it out loud so that he could remember it. 'Adam.'

'Right.'

They smiled at each other for a second.

Okay, I don't care. He is very attractive.

Georgie wondered why he worked shifts. Maybe it was just the nosey copper in her. 'What do you do, Adam?'

'I'm a paramedic.'

Attractive paramedic. Nice.

'Oh right,' she said with an interested tone. 'Based at University Hospital in town then?'

He nodded. 'That's right. I worked over in Manchester for a few years. That's where I'm from. But I just fancied a change.' There were a few seconds of silence.

Adam had hesitated over his phrase *But I just fancied a change* but Georgie knew that it wasn't the time or place to ask him why he'd fancied a change.

'And what do you do, Georgie?' he asked with a slightly nervous laugh as having asked the same question back to her.

'Police officer,' she said with an element of pride. 'Detective. Actually detective constable.'

Oh my God, why am I babbling?

'Oh right.' Adam definitely looked impressed but also slightly confused. 'God, that's a tough job.'

'No more than being a paramedic, I imagine,' Georgie said, and then gestured to her car. 'Right, I'd better get going or I'll be late.'

Adam looked directly at her. 'Nice to have met you, Georgie.' He seemed to really mean it.

She quickly glanced at his left hand. No wedding ring. *Interesting.*

Okay, Georgie, play it nice and cool. Get in the car and drive away.

'You too.' She gave him her best smile, got into the car, started the ignition and slowly reversed off the drive.

Looking up, she saw that he was watching her so she gave him a little wave. He waved back.

Chapter 4

Ruth was sitting in her office. Opposite sat Detective Constable Alfie Price – early 20s, mousy brown hair, round friendly face and a button nose - who had just joined CID after three years in uniform over in Prestatyn. Like all CID officers, Price would be on a three-month trial after which Ruth would make an assessment as to his suitability to continue in Llancastell CID.

'Where are you originally from, Alfie?' she asked as she peered down at his personnel file.

'Prestatyn born and bred,' he said proudly.

Although he was articulate and personable, Ruth also felt that he seemed incredibly young. Maybe she was just getting old. She remembered the old adage about police officers looking younger and younger. Looking down at his file, she saw that he was only 23 years old. He was younger than her daughter Ella.

'Did you join with a view to working in CID?' Ruth asked.

'Yes, that was my plan,' Price replied. 'My father is a copper.'

She raised an eyebrow. 'CID?'

'Oh no.' Price shook his head. 'Uniform. He's a custody sergeant in Rhyl.'

Ruth frowned. 'What's his name?'

'John.'

'John Price. Don't think I've met him since I came up this way. I was in the Met for many years.'

Price looked at her. 'I didn't like to say, but you don't sound like you come from North Wales, ma'am.'

'It's boss, never ma'am,' she said in a friendly tone. 'And no. I'm Battersea born and bred.'

Price shrugged. 'I don't know where that is. I've only been to London twice.'

'Well, you're not missing much,' Ruth said dryly. 'That's why I'm up here.' Then she got up and went to her office door and looked over at Detective Constable Jade Kennedy, who had only recently joined them from Chester. 'Jade, can I borrow you for a moment?'

'Yes, boss,' Kennedy said with a quizzical look on her face.

Price stood up.

'Jade, this is Alfie,' Ruth said by way of an introduction. 'First week in CID so I'm going to ask you to team up with him and show him the ropes.'

'No problem,' Kennedy said. Ruth couldn't work out if Kennedy was annoyed about being lumbered with a 'newbie'. She didn't care. It was all part of the job, and if Kennedy wanted to progress up the ranks of CID – as Ruth suspected she did – then part of that job was to work with new officers.

'Right, that's sorted then,' Ruth said brightly. 'Jade, can you show Alfie where his desk is and get him logged on?'

'Of course,' she said, and beckoned for Price to follow her.

Ruth slumped down in her chair and let out a sigh. Then she clocked the mountain of paperwork on her desk and her heart sank.

For a moment, her eyes rested again on a photograph of her partner Sarah, and Daniel, who was eleven years old. Ruth and Sarah had got a temporary fostering licence to look after Daniel after his father died. In fact, Daniel had been living with them for several months now and they felt like a lovely family unit. Six weeks ago, the paperwork for his permanent adoption had been signed. However, he had been kidnapped before being dramatically rescued up on the North Wales coast at the Great Orme. He had been targeted as a way of getting to Ruth. Social services had put a hold on Ruth and Sarah's permanent adoption of Daniel as they needed to do a thorough review and risk assessment to see if Ruth's job could ever put him in danger again. Waiting for them to reach their conclusion was making Ruth and Sarah jittery.

DS Nick Evans knocked on the open door and looked in.

'I know. I'm coming,' Ruth said, assuming that he had appeared to remind her that the CID team was waiting for her to come and take the morning briefing.

Getting up from her desk, she felt her knees click loudly.

Bloody hell, I really am getting old, she thought to herself as she grabbed her coffee and files.

'It's not that, boss,' Nick said.

'What do you mean?'

'We've had a call from Merseyside Police,' he explained.

Ruth frowned, none the wiser. 'Okay.'

'They've found a body in a burned out car over in Heswall on The Wirral.'

Ruth shrugged. 'Right. And what's that got to do with us?' she asked, aware that she was sounding a little grumpy this morning. She had planned to spend the day getting through the interminable paperwork that had built up in recent weeks.

'The car and the registered owner are from Wrexham,' Nick replied, 'so it falls under our jurisdiction.'

'Okay,' Ruth said, realising that now she'd have to change her plans. She then gestured to the office. 'Quick briefing and then we'd better get over there to see what's happened.'

'Yes, boss.'

As Ruth went out into the CID office, she saw that a member of the team was missing. She narrowed her eyes as she looked at Nick.

'Any sign of Jim?' she asked.

Nick shook his head. 'Not yet, boss.'

She glanced at her watch. It was 9.04am. Garrow was never late, and given all that had happened to him over the dropped charges against Lucy Morgan, and his possible disciplinary, it made her feel uneasy.

'Give him a call to check he's okay, would you?' Ruth asked as she strode across the CID office.

Chapter 5

Garrow blinked open his eyes and felt a sharp pain at the front of his head. He squinted up at the ceiling and realised that he was lying on the sofa in his living room. And he was fully clothed.

For a few seconds, he thought he was going to vomit. He took a long, deep breath to try and steady himself. As he rolled onto his side, he spotted the nearly empty bottle of Jack Daniel's resting on the coffee table. Then it all came flooding back to him.

Oh my God! he thought as an overwhelming wave of panic swept over him. *I think I killed Lucy Morgan last night.*

Trying to sit up, he realised that he was indeed going to vomit. He dashed to the downstairs toilet. Then he splashed his face with cold water and looked at his reflection in the mirror. He looked terrible. Drawn, puffy, tired. His eyes were bloodshot. He studied the face that looked back at him. What the hell had happened to him in the past few days? His life seemed to have been trundling along at a nice, steady pace. Then bam. Everything in his life had been turned upside down. The dropped charges. The pending disciplinary hearing in which he could lose his job. And now the stomach-churning reality that he had deliberately run his car into Lucy Morgan last night, killed her and then driven away.

Who the hell are you? the little voice in his head asked as he stared at his reflection.

As his stomach started to settle and his thoughts gathered, he checked his watch. It was 9.40am! *Jesus! Bloody hell! I've missed briefing and I haven't even called in sick.*

The anxiety and despondency were now crippling. He knew that what he needed to do was shower, change, drink a strong coffee and head into Llancastell CID. But there was another nagging voice that told him to hide away.

Stumbling back to the living room, he fell back onto the sofa. Blowing out his cheeks, he shook his head as he reached over for the Jack Daniel's. He couldn't believe that he was about to have another drink but he also couldn't face reality.

Screwing up his face and holding his breath, he took three big glugs of whiskey and then closed his eyes. He could feel its heat at the back of his throat and then down in his stomach.

He waited, and it wasn't long before he got a slightly numb, tingling feeling as the alcohol began to zip its way through his bloodstream and calm his nervous system.

Thank God for that. Now I can concentrate.

Grabbing his phone, he went immediately onto various local news sites. He wanted to see if there had been a fatal hit and run reported anywhere. After five minutes of scouring *The Leader*, *North Wales Post* and others, he saw that the story wasn't being reported. Yet.

He reached over for the TV remote control. Skipping through the various channels, he found a local radio station which he put on. He could listen to the news at 10am to see if it was carrying the story.

Then suddenly something occurred to him.

The car! Jesus, the bloody car!

He stood up, marched down the hallway and opened the front door.

Taking a few tentative steps towards his car, he looked down at the front bumper.

On the left hand side, there were two dents in the bodywork. There was also a crack and marks on the bumper itself.

Crouching down, he glanced around to make sure that none of his neighbours were watching.

He carefully inspected the damage.

Then he saw something on the paintwork. Dark circular flecks.

It was blood.

Chapter 6

As Ruth and Nick headed north from Llancastell towards The Wirral, Ruth took out her phone.

'No answer from Jim?' she asked, glancing over at Nick.

'Just went to voicemail,' he explained and then frowned. 'I've never known him miss a day since he started.'

'Yeah, that's what worries me,' Ruth admitted as they joined the A550 heading for Deeside.

Nick raised a quizzical eyebrow. 'He's got that disciplinary hanging over his head.'

'And that bloody Lucy Morgan had been stalking him,' Ruth said, thinking out loud. 'You think we should go and check on him or send someone round?'

'Maybe.' Nick shrugged. 'It's definitely out of character for him not to turn up to work and not to let someone know.'

For a few seconds, Ruth looked out of the car window. She needed to smoke. Taking a packet of cigarettes from her coat pocket, she pulled one out and popped it between her lips. Smoking would help her think. She was definitely worried about Garrow.

Buzzing down the window, she lit the cigarette, took a long deep drag and then blew a plume of bluish smoke out and watched as the wind snatched it and took it away.

The sunshine glared down from a cloudless, perfect sky. Ruth took out her sunglasses and put them on before taking another drag on the cigarette.

Hearing the refrain from a song on the radio, she leaned over and turned it up. It was *Back for Good* by *Take That*.

'I was about to turn that off,' Nick groaned.

'This is a classic,' Ruth protested.

'Come on.' Nick gave her a withering look. '*Take That*? Really? I didn't think that even you would stoop that low.'

Ruth gave him a look of mock indignation. 'Sometimes Nicholas, you can be very rude. Especially as I'm the senior ranking officer in this car.'

'I read an article a few weeks ago comparing Gary Barlow to Elton John and George Michael,' Nick said, shaking his head. 'There's no comparison. Some of that early Elton John is great. *Rocket Man, Yellow Brick Road* and even before that. When he was living in LA and hanging out with John Lennon and Harry Nilsson in the Troubadour. That's when he wrote his best stuff.'

Ruth gave Nick a wry smile. 'You know what I realised?'

'What?'

'I can sleep with my eyes open,' she said sardonically.

Nick forced a sarcastic grin. 'Very funny.'

Ruth laughed. 'Don't be offended. I love it that you're a total music bore. It's very … endearing.'

'Endearing? Jesus. You make it sound like I have 'special needs'.'

'If the cap fits,' Ruth joked. Her phone rang, interrupting their joking around.

She saw that the call was coming from Llancastell CID.

'DI Hunter?' she said.

'Boss?' came a voice that she recognised.

It was Kennedy.

'Yes, Jade?'

'We've got a report coming in of a hit and run from last night.'

'Okay,' Ruth said with a frown. 'Probably something for uniform to look at to start with, Jade.'

'Yes, boss. The only thing is that the victim was Lucy Morgan. And she was seriously injured. She's in Llancastell University Hospital Critical Care Unit.'

'Right,' Ruth said as her stomach tightened with anxiety. She hoped to God that Garrow's disappearing act today and the hit and run weren't connected. However, her instinct told her that they were. And that was terrible news for everyone at Llancastell CID. 'Has Jim come into work yet or let someone know where he is?'

'No, boss. I'll let you know as soon as he does.'

'Okay,' Ruth said. 'Can you get as much information about the hit and run as you can and we'll deal with it when we get back?'

'Yes, boss,' Kennedy said as she ended the call.

Nick gave Ruth a quizzical look. 'Everything okay?'

'Not really. Lucy Morgan was involved in a hit and run last night. She's in a critical condition in the CCU. And Jim hasn't arrived at work and isn't answering his phone. I can't believe that it's coincidence.'

'No,' Nick agreed. 'Neither can I.'

Chapter 7

Taking a wet cloth and a bucket, Garrow crouched down on the driveway in front of his car. He'd checked a few times to make sure that none of his neighbours were around. Soaking the cloth, he rubbed away the blood on his paintwork and bumper.

Christ, I can't believe that I'm actually doing this.

After about a minute, he was satisfied that the blood was now gone. However, he'd been a detective long enough to know that if a forensics team were examining it, there would be microscopic particles of blood that just weren't visible to the human eye. He prayed to God that it didn't come to that.

Taking out a small tack hammer, he stood up and looked up and down the road again, trying to look as nonchalant as possible. Even though he'd had a few swigs of whiskey, his anxiety was through the roof. However, the pain in his head had gone now.

Crouching down again, he tried to use the tack hammer to knock the two dents out of the bodywork to the side of the bumper. The metallic bangs of his hammer against the steel seemed to reverberate around the whole area.

Jesus, that's loud, he thought anxiously.

As he continued to tap away, hoping that eventually the dents would disappear, he tried to rack his brains. Did the Cross Foxes pub have any CCTV in their rear car park? He didn't think they did. At least he hadn't noticed any and he was usually pretty good at spotting stuff like that. It was a by-product of being a detective.

However, if there was CCTV out in the car park, he was screwed. His number plate would probably be visible as he drove into Lucy Morgan. His plate would be checked with the DVLA and that would lead police officers to his door. He wasn't quite sure why he was bothering to clean his car and try to knock out the dents. But he felt that he needed to be doing something.

'Bit a problem there, Jim?' said a voice that made him jump out of his skin.

'Bloody hell!' Garrow said as he looked up and saw his elderly neighbour Bob looking down at him.

Bob laughed. 'Sorry, did I make you jump?'

Garrow stood up. 'It's fine. I was miles away.'

'What happened?' Bob asked as he pointed to the dents that Garrow was trying to remove with the tack hammer.

Garrow thought for a moment. *Well Bob, I deliberately drove my car into a young woman while I was drunk last night and I'm pretty sure she's dead.*

'Someone must have reversed into me while I was parked in a car park somewhere yesterday,' he explained.

Bob raised an eyebrow. 'Didn't leave a note?'

'No,' Garrow replied, hoping that Bob would go soon. His presence was making his anxiety worse.

'Don't know what the world is coming to,' Bob said,

shaking his head, 'but of course you'd know about that, Jim, wouldn't you?'

'Yes.'

'Not at work today?'

'I'm on nights this week,' he lied.

'Right you are,' Bob said, and then pointed to the car again. 'You're probably going to need a bodyshop to get that out for you.'

'Yeah, I think I'll do that,' Garrow said as he watched Bob wander away.

Chapter 8

It was mid-morning by the time Ruth and Nick arrived at the Headline Properties development site in Heswall on The Wirral. The site had been cordoned off with blue and white police evidence tape, and two patrol cars had been pulled across the entrance to prevent any vehicles entering.

As Nick stopped the car, a uniformed police officer – 30s, male, thick-set and wearing a high-vis police jacket – approached and looked at them.

Ruth and Nick took out their warrant cards as Nick buzzed down the window.

'Can I help, sir?' the officer asked politely.

'DS Evans and DI Hunter, North Wales Police,' Nick explained. 'We had a call to meet a DI Gorski here?'

'Yes, sir,' the officer said as he grabbed his police Tetra radio. 'I'll let DI Gorksi know that you've arrived.'

'Thank you, constable,' Nick said as the officer moved away and they drove into the site.

There were five newly-built houses that looked like they were close to being finished.

Over to the right, there was a SOCO forensic van with

its back doors open. A couple of SOCOs in full forensic gear – white nitrile suit, hat, mask and white rubber boots – were milling around and putting forensic evidence into the van.

Over to the left, there was the burned out shell of what looked to be a car of some kind but it was impossible to determine what make of car it was. The shell of the car was still smouldering and there were still several fire officers in maroon and yellow suits and hard hats standing and talking nearby.

Ruth and Nick parked and got out. The air was thick with the smell of burning rubber and metal.

A woman in a forensic suit approached.

'DI Hunter, DS Evans?' she asked with a thick Scouse accent.

'DI Gorski?' Ruth asked, assuming their arrival had been relayed to her.

'That's right. Thanks for coming over,' she said as she pulled down her mask. She was in her late 30s, blonde, thin, and had an attractive face with a small line of freckles across her nose. She gestured towards the burned out car. 'Do you want to follow me?'

'Yes, of course,' Ruth replied.

'I'll get you some shoe covers,' Gorski said.

'What have we got so far?' Ruth asked as they headed towards some SOCOs who would provide her and Nick with the forensic shoe covers. If they needed to go closer to the car, they would need to wear full forensic gear.

'Builders arrived to start work at 8am. The main gates to the site were open and they found the car still smouldering,' Gorski explained as she handed the shoe covers to Ruth and Nick. 'At first, they thought the car had been stolen, abandoned and then burned. We get a lot of that around here. But then they saw that there was a body lying across the back seat.'

'Any way of identifying the body?' Nick asked.

Gorski shook her head with a grim expression. 'The fire was too intense. But the car is registered to a Martin Jones in Wrexham. We've got an address. Obviously, that's why you're here.'

'Anyone tried to reach him?' Ruth asked.

'I've spoken to his wife, Steph,' Gorski explained. 'She said that he left the house early to go to the gym. About 6am. She hasn't heard from him since.'

Ruth looked at Nick. 'Can you get onto Georgie? Get her to go over to the address in Wrexham in case Martin Jones turns up there.'

'Yes, boss,' Nick said as he walked away and took out his phone.

An older Asian man in a forensic suit, who had been taking photographs of the car, came over.

'DI Hunter, this is our chief pathologist for The Wirral area, Professor Gupta,' Gorski explained.

'Pretty grisly for a summer's morning,' Gupta said dryly.

'What can you tell us?' Gorksi asked.

'Adult male between twenty and forty,' he replied. 'Approximate height, around five foot ten.'

'Nothing else?' Gorski asked, sounding impatient.

'There are five or even six severe injuries to the side and back of the skull. They do look recent, so my assumption is that the victim was subjected to a very violent attack before being put in the car.'

'This morning?' Ruth asked. 'Given that the car is still smouldering.'

'Probably.' Gupta shrugged. 'The victim will be taken to Llancastell University Hospital, so it will be Professor

Amis who carries out the post-mortem. We'll know more after that.'

Ruth gestured to the burned out car. 'Forensics aren't going to be able to get a lot from that.'

'No.' Gorski nodded and raised an eyebrow. 'Which is probably why they set fire to the car. Fire inspectors have confirmed that it was set on fire deliberately.'

'Do we have any idea of time of death?' Nick asked as he rejoined them.

'No more than a few hours from the looks of it,' Gupta said.

Ruth nodded. 'I just hope that whoever it was, they were dead before the fire in that car started.'

'If you're in agreement, I'm now treating this as a murder investigation,' Gorski said.

Ruth was pleased to see that Gorski was asking her opinion.

She nodded. 'Looks that way to me.'

'If you guys could go and talk to Steph Jones,' Gorski suggested, 'I can carry on here. If that works?'

'Yes, no problem,' Ruth said, pleasantly surprised at Gorski's manner. Her recent experience of working with the police in Chester had made her wary of this type of joint investigation so she hoped this time it would be different.

Chapter 9

Ruth and Nick pulled up outside a small detached house in Gresford, an affluent suburb of Wrexham. The house was newly-built with a tidy, well-kept front garden. There was a child's plastic scooter, an orange football and various other toys on the lawn, but no sign of any children.

As they got out of the car, Georgie opened the front door to the house and approached. Ruth had arranged for her to act as the family liaison officer (FLO) for the Jones family. Ruth had seen Georgie put herself in enough precarious situations while she was pregnant so she was trying to make sure that she gave her jobs that didn't put her in any danger.

'How's she doing in there?' she asked as Georgie came over.

'They're all very anxious,' Georgie explained, pulling a face.

'Not surprising.'

Nick glanced over at the toys. 'How many children do they have?'

'Three. All under ten.' She gestured to the house next

door. 'They've gone to play with the neighbour's kids. Martin's sister Lilly is in there with Steph.'

They all headed for the front door.

'What have you told her?' Ruth asked.

'I just said that you'd found Martin's car on The Wirral. Nothing else yet, boss.'

'Good.'

Entering the hallway, Ruth could see that the house was tidy, clean and fashionably decorated. There was a row of hooks with assorted raincoats and scarves. Underneath that, a row of shoes and wellies. The house smelled of freshly brewed coffee.

Georgie pointed to a door that was half open. 'They're in the living room.'

Ruth pushed the door open fully and saw two women in their 30s sitting next to each other on the large, cream-coloured sofa. They both looked very scared.

'Have you found him?' asked the woman with red hair, sharp cheekbones and blue eyes. 'Have you found Martin?'

Ruth looked at her with a calm expression. 'I'm Detective Inspector Ruth Hunter and this is Detective Sergeant Nick Evans. We're from Llancastell CID. I didn't catch your name?'

'Steph,' she said as she got up from the sofa and paced the room frantically.

'And Martin Jones is your husband, is that right?'

'Yes,' she said a little snappily. 'I just need to know if you've found him. Why aren't you telling me what's going on?'

'I'm going to need you to sit down please, Steph,' Ruth said very gently as she gestured to the sofa.

Steph looked at her.

'Please,' Ruth repeated.

Steph sat down next to Lilly and leaned forward.

Ruth went over to an armchair and sat down opposite them.

'Now I know that DC Wild here has informed you that your husband's car was found over on The Wirral, and that it had been burned out,' Ruth said calmly.

'Yes,' Steph said, her voice shaky.

'I'm sorry to tell you that we also found a body on the back seat of that car,' Ruth said quietly.

'Oh my God,' Steph cried out, putting her hand to her mouth in shock.

The woman who Ruth assumed was Martin's sister, Lilly, frowned as she looked up at her in horror. She had brunette hair pulled back off her face and wore glasses. 'No,' she gasped as she shook her head in disbelief.

'But at the moment we don't know if it's Martin,' Nick said, trying to calm them both.

'Why not?' Lilly asked with a confused expression.

Ruth knew that this wasn't going to be an easy thing to explain to them. 'Martin's car had suffered significant damage as it had been burned out.'

'Oh no,' Steph said as she burst into tears. Lilly took her hand to comfort her.

'Now we don't know who it is on the back seat,' Ruth continued. 'The car could have been stolen.'

Steph shook her head as she wiped the tears from her face. 'My husband works on The Wirral at the moment. I know it's him.'

Ruth leaned forward in the armchair. 'Until we know for certain, I think we need to try and stay positive. I know that's very difficult under these circumstances. And we are going to need to ask you some questions, okay?'

Steph took a deep breath to try to compose herself. 'Yes.'

Nick sat down and then took a notepad and pen from his jacket pocket.

'Can you tell us the last time you saw Martin?' Ruth enquired.

'This morning. It was early and he went out to the gym,' Steph replied.

Nick looked over. 'And what time would that have been?'

'Six. Six thirty. I was still in bed but I heard him get up and go.'

'And you're sure that he was going to the gym?'

'Yes. He goes every morning. Like clockwork. He laid out his gym clothes and packed his bag last night like he always does.'

'And what gym does he go to?'

'Total Fitness in Wrexham.'

Nick narrowed his eyes. 'How had Martin been recently? Was there anything going on that was worrying him ... anything out of the ordinary?'

Lilly shrugged. 'He was building some houses in Heswall over on The Wirral which might have been stressful. But to be fair, he said that it was going really well.'

Steph nodded. 'Everything was going well for us.' Then she seemed overcome again with fear and her eyes filled with tears.

Nick looked from one to the other. 'Was there anyone who might want to harm Martin? Any disputes or arguments recently, either personal or professional?'

Lilly and Steph both shook their heads.

'No,' Steph whispered. 'Nothing like that.'

'Can you tell us if he had an office that he worked out of?'

'Yeah,' Lilly confirmed, 'he rented offices in the middle of Wrexham. Above a bar in High Street.'

'Okay, thank you,' Ruth said. 'Detective Constable Wild here is going to stay with you. And she'll let you know as soon as there are any developments.' She paused for a second and then added gently, 'I'm sorry to ask, but I am going to need something of Martin's. A toothbrush or comb ... for DNA.'

Steph nodded but she looked crushed. 'Of course.'

Chapter 10

Ruth and Nick walked into the reception of Total Fitness in Wrexham. A young woman in her 20s – black hair, attractive – looked up and gave them a cheesy smile.

'Hi there,' she said in an overly chirpy voice. 'Can I help you?'

Ruth didn't like to say that she'd actually had a membership to Total Fitness gyms for over two years and had only used it six times. So could she cancel her membership?

'Hi … DI Ruth Hunter and DS Nick Evans,' she said as she flashed her warrant card. 'Llancastell CID. We need to check if one of your members was at the gym this morning.'

'Oh right.' The woman immediately looked concerned. 'I might need to talk to my manager.'

'Listen, this is a murder investigation,' Ruth explained politely, 'so I'm going to need that information right now. We don't have time for you to talk to your manager.'

The woman's face fell and she nodded. 'Erm, yes. Of

course, sorry,' she babbled uncertainly. 'Could you tell me the member's name please?'

'Martin Jones,' Nick said.

'Martin Jones?' the woman asked with a concerned frown.

Nick raised an eyebrow. 'Do you know him?'

'Yes. I went to school with his brother. And I see him when he comes in here. Is he all right?'

Ruth looked at her blankly. 'We just need to know if he was in the gym this morning at any point?'

'Yes, of course,' the woman said as she went to the computer and started to tap away at the keyboard. Then she shook her head. 'No. Martin hasn't been in for a few months.'

'Really?' Ruth said. Steph Jones had said that he came to the gym every morning.

The woman pointed to the screen. 'No. He hasn't been in since May.'

'And there's no way that he could have come into the gym this morning, or any other time, without it showing up on your system?' Ruth asked, gesturing to the computer.

'No. Members have wristbands which they have to use to get in,' she explained. 'And that records the information on our system. There's no way that Martin has been in the gym during the last few weeks.'

Ruth shot a quizzical look at Nick. Martin Jones had definitely lied to his wife about where he'd been going.

Chapter 11

Ruth and Nick arrived at Headline Properties which was located above a popular bar called *Vault 33* on High Street in the centre of Wrexham. Having explained who they were, they had been buzzed in and were now going up the narrow staircase to the first floor. The air smelled of recently hoovered carpets and fresh coffee. Framed photos of luxury houses had been hung in a neat line on the wall up the stairs.

As they got to the top, there was what looked like a reception area and a big sign, *Headline Properties*, on the wall. A woman in her late 40s with short, blonde hair and glasses sat behind a large desk with a computer in front of her. However, she looked concerned. Ruth had informed her that they were from Llancastell CID, which made most people feel uneasy.

'Hi there,' Ruth said as she and Nick showed their warrant cards. 'We understand that Martin Jones works here.'

The woman nodded. 'He's one of the owners but he's not in yet.'

At that moment, another woman in her 30s, jet black hair, designer business suit approached.

'Hi, I'm Ruby Allen,' she said confidently. 'I'm Martin's business partner here.

Is there something wrong?'

'I'm afraid that Martin's car was found over on The Wirral this morning,' Ruth said calmly.

Ruby looked confused. 'I don't understand.'

'Is there somewhere a little more private we can go?' Ruth said.

Ruby nodded and gestured. 'Do you want to come through to my office?'

'Yes, thank you,' Nick replied.

Holding open the door for them, Ruby then turned left and led them down a smart corridor and into a corner office. It was stylishly furnished with large windows. There were various awards and certificates in frames on the walls.

'Please, sit down,' Ruby said as she went over to her desk.

Ruth looked at her. 'I'm afraid that Martin's car was discovered burned out at your development site in Heswall … and a body was discovered in the back of the vehicle.'

Ruby gasped as she looked at them. 'Oh my God, is it Martin?'

'We don't know yet,' Ruth said. 'The fire did a lot of damage.'

Ruby let out a breath and shook her head. 'Oh God, that's terrible.'

'I take it you've had no contact with Martin this morning?' Nick asked.

'No.' Ruby shook her head. 'When he didn't turn up for work, I tried calling his mobile phone but it went straight to voicemail.'

As she moved a strand of hair from her face, Ruth noticed a very shiny charm bracelet on her left wrist.

Nick took out his pen and notepad. 'The thing is, Martin told his wife that he was going to the gym. But we've checked and he hasn't been to the gym in a couple of months.'

Ruby shrugged. 'Sorry, I don't know anything about that.'

Nick continued. 'It does mean that Martin drove over to your site in Heswall very early this morning. Do you have any idea why?'

'No, I don't.' Ruby looked confused, then she pointed at her computer. 'I can check his diary if that helps?'

'Please,' Ruth replied. She spotted a photograph on the desk showing Ruby with a teenage boy who looked about eighteen.

Ruby tapped at her keyboard, then peered at the screen and shook her head. 'No. There's nothing in the diary, and I can't think of any reason why Martin would be over there.' Then she looked upset. 'I can't believe this is happening.'

'How long have you been working together?' Nick asked.

'Martin and I set up Headline Properties just over three years ago,' she explained.

Ruth raised an eyebrow. 'And everything has been going well?'

'Yes, very well. In fact, better than we ever thought it would.'

'Can you tell us the last time you saw or had any contact with Martin?'

Ruby took a couple of seconds. 'I didn't speak to him yesterday as I was out of the office all day. So it must have been the day before that, I think.'

Nick scratched at his beard and asked, 'Can you think of anyone who might want to harm Martin?'

'No,' Ruby replied adamantly. 'Martin can be a bit abrasive sometimes, and he doesn't suffer fools, but I can't think of anyone who would want to hurt him.'

Ruth frowned. She assumed that property development wasn't without its challenges. 'No arguments or disputes with anyone?'

Ruby thought about it for a moment as something occurred to her.

'Go on,' Ruth prompted her. 'However insignificant you think it might be, we need to know.'

'We had an accident on that site about a year ago. A workman, Andy Fletcher, fell from a cherry picker crane and died. He wasn't wearing his safety harness properly. There was an industrial tribunal and enquiry but there were no charges of negligence against us. But Andy's wife, Sonia, maintains that Martin forced Andy to go up in the crane even though the weather was bad.'

Ruth narrowed her eyes. 'Did he?'

Ruby shook her head. 'Not as far as I know. Martin was adamant that Andy was happy to go up there. It was just a terrible accident, but Sonia Fletcher just doesn't see it like that. In fact, she's spent the last year doing everything she can to discredit Martin. Online campaigns. She's been to journalists, her local MP.'

'Anything more sinister than that?' Ruth asked.

'I don't think so.'

Ruth gave Nick a look. It sounded as if the accident might be significant to their investigation.

Chapter 12

An hour later, Ruth and Nick were sitting in the waiting area of the Critical Care Unit of Llancastell University Hospital. Even though they had a murder case on their hands, Ruth was scared that Garrow was somehow involved in what had happened to Lucy. She wanted to be in control of any investigation so she could limit any damage to one of her officers.

Twenty minutes earlier a call had come through from a doctor to say that Lucy Morgan had regained consciousness, and although she was groggy, she was talking and lucid. Ruth was surprised given that the last they'd heard, she was critical. She knew it was vital that she find out what Lucy remembered about the previous evening, if she'd seen the driver of the car that hit her, and if that person was Jim Garrow.

Looking up, she saw that a young male doctor was approaching.

'Detective Inspector Hunter?' he asked.

'Yes,' Ruth replied as they got up. 'How is Lucy doing?'

There was a large part of her that resented having to

enquire about Lucy Morgan's health at all. She had brutally killed her own mother in cold blood and then manipulated and hounded Garrow. If she was honest, Ruth felt that the world would be a better place without someone like Lucy Morgan roaming around causing mayhem.

'She's remarkably well, all things considered,' the doctor admitted. 'CT scans show no internal bleeding or damage to her brain. Just a couple of cracked ribs. Could have been a lot worse. She's very lucky.'

I wish it had been a lot worse, Ruth thought to herself.

'Can we talk to her?' Nick asked.

'Yes. But if you can make it brief please. She's very tired from the pain medication.'

'Of course,' Ruth reassured him through gritted teeth.

They followed him through the secure doors into the Critical Care Unit and he gestured to the door of Lucy's room. 'She's just in there.'

'Thank you,' Nick said.

Opening the door, they went in and saw that Lucy was hooked up to an ECG, as well as an IV drip.

Lucy sensed their presence and turned her head slowly to look at them.

'Oh hello,' she croaked with a cheery smile. 'What a lovely surprise.' It sounded as if she was greeting old friends.

She really is a very strange and dangerous young woman, Ruth thought to herself.

'Hello Lucy,' she said calmly. 'I'm Detective Inspector Hunter and this is Detective Sergeant Evans. We're from Llancastell CID.'

Lucy nodded. 'Yes, I know. I remember you from when there was an investigation into my poor mother's death.'

I think you mean your mother's brutal murder which you committed? Ruth thought.

'Okay if we sit down?' Nick asked as he gestured to a couple of red plastic chairs that were close to the bed.

'Be my guest,' Lucy said with a smile.

Ruth sat down and looked at her. She found Lucy's overly friendly manner very unnerving.

'Do you know that you were involved in an accident last night?' she asked.

Lucy nodded but frowned. 'That's what the nurses and doctors told me, but I can't seem to remember anything.'

Nick raised an eyebrow. 'You don't remember anything at all?'

She shook her head and pulled a face. 'No, sorry. I don't remember a thing about the accident.'

'You were found unconscious at the entrance to the car park at the Cross Foxes pub in Erbistock,' Ruth explained. 'Does that ring any bells?'

'Right,' Lucy said as she furrowed her brow. 'Yes.'

'Do you remember being at that pub?' Nick enquired.

'Yes, vaguely. I'd met a friend of mine there for a drink.'

Nick, who had now pulled out his notebook and pen, asked, 'Could you tell us who you met there?'

'His name is Adam.'

'Adam …?' Nick said, implying that he needed a surname.

Lucy giggled. 'Oh God, sorry. I've no idea. He's not a friend actually. We met via an online site. You know a 'hook up' thing?'

Ruth nodded to show that she knew what Lucy was talking about.

'It didn't go very well, to be honest,' Lucy continued. 'I took one look at him and thought 'No thanks'. He had weird teeth for starters. And I think his profile picture was taken about ten years ago. Classic.' She laughed and shook her head.

'Can you tell us what happened after you'd met Adam?' Ruth asked.

'I made my excuses and decided to leave,' Lucy said, and then she furrowed her brow. 'And then I'm afraid it's all a bit of a blank.'

'We believe that you were hit by a car. Possibly coming out of the car park.'

'No,' Lucy said, shaking her head. 'I just can't remember anything until I woke up here.'

Ruth shot Nick a look. If Garrow had been involved in Lucy's hit and run, then he might have had a very lucky escape. Not only was she alive, but at the moment she couldn't remember a thing.

Ruth just prayed that Lucy's memory didn't come back.

Chapter 13

Ruth was standing in the kitchen staring out of the window as she waited for Daniel's frozen margherita pizza to 'cook' in the oven. It had been a long and stressful day. She was aware that she now craved a cigarette but she was going to put that off until Daniel had gone to bed. He got angry when she smoked and so she had to sneak down the side of the house to smoke by the bins when she was really desperate. Daniel said that smoking was really bad for her and that it could kill her. Obviously Ruth was fully aware of that. But given her job, she was also aware that there were many things out there that could kill anyone. And often people died very suddenly. So, in her head, she wanted to keep the one pleasure she had in life – smoking. Even if it was selfish and illogical.

'Is it ready yet, bro?' asked a voice.

It was Daniel. He was wearing a baseball cap. In fact, these days he was always wearing a baseball cap of some kind.

'Hey,' Ruth said with a smile. She went over and

wrapped her arms around him but felt him resist a little. 'What's wrong?' she asked as she let him go.

'You smell of smoke,' he groaned.

Ruth hadn't yet changed since she came in from work and she'd had at least four or five cigarettes in the car with Nick.

'Sorry. Guilty as charged,' she said with an apologetic grin.

'It's not funny,' Daniel said, wagging his finger at her and shaking his head.

Ruth leaned down and looked into the oven. 'I reckon another five minutes before it's ready, bro. Do you want some salad with your pizza?'

Daniel looked bewildered. 'Erm, no. I'm not a freak.'

Ruth gave him a bemused look. 'Eating salad doesn't make you a freak.'

'Yeah, it does,' he protested.

'Some cucumber as a compromise?' she suggested.

'I'll have some waffles as a compromise.'

'Yeah, I'm not sure that frozen waffles actually count as salad, Daniel.'

'Oh well.' He shrugged and then looked at her. 'Have you heard back from that adoption lady yet?'

'No,' Ruth said. 'They're dragging their feet a bit so I'll give them a call tomorrow, okay?'

Daniel looked worried.

She went over to him and placed her hands on his shoulders. 'Hey, don't worry. It's going to be fine. It's just the usual red tape.'

Daniel frowned. 'What does 'red tape' mean?'

'Erm ... it means that there's lots of complicated forms and paperwork for them to look through and sign. And that's why it takes so long.'

'Oh, right,' Daniel said as he turned and strolled away.

For a moment, Ruth imagined what would happen if social services actually blocked her and Sarah's application to permanently adopt Daniel. She couldn't even bring herself to think about it. The idea of him moving out just broke her heart.

Chapter 14

Garrow was sitting on the sofa with the lights turned off. The television was still tuned in to BBC Radio Wales but there had been no reports of Lucy's death or any hit and run accidents. Earlier he'd trawled the local news sites on his phone but there was still nothing.

He'd managed to keep his drinking to a minimum during the day but he was feeling tired, sick and anxious. Looking at his watch he saw that it was 8pm. In anyone's books it was a normal time to have a drink. Sniffing at his clothes, he knew that he needed to shower and change.

Wandering into the kitchen, he grabbed a tumbler and looked around. The kitchen was a mess. Even though he had a dishwasher, he just didn't have the inclination to stack it. His kitchen was usually spotless so it was horrible to look at it like this.

Taking a bottle of red wine, which was now the only alcohol he had left in the house, he screwed the top off and poured himself a huge tumbler. He wasn't sure why he hadn't used a proper wine glass. He supposed that he just wasn't thinking clearly.

As he ambled back to the living room, he tried to work out why no police officers had called at his house. He had to assume that there were no CCTV cameras at the Cross Foxes pub and therefore no one could know that he'd been the one to kill Lucy. That was the only explanation, he hoped.

Suddenly there was a knock on the door.

Garrow froze. Reaching for the remote control, he turned off the television and sat down on the sofa. The living room was now plunged into darkness.

Whoever was at the door, knocked again. This time more urgently and louder.

Shit! Maybe it's police officers? Maybe it's taken them this long to track me down.

He felt sick with fear.

Then he heard his letterbox open.

'Jim? Jim?' called a familiar voice.

It was Nick from work.

'Jim? Are you there, mate? Just let me in would you?' he called through the letterbox.

Getting up from the sofa, Garrow padded slowly towards the front window which was covered by drawn curtains.

Silence.

Then he heard the sound of the letterbox being closed.

Pulling back the curtain by about a centimetre, he peered outside.

Nick had taken a few steps back down the garden path and was looking up at the house.

Then he turned and headed back to his car.

Garrow let the curtain close.

Chapter 15

Ruth took a long, deep drag on her cigarette and then blew the smoke up into the night sky. It was nearly dark and the evenings were getting shorter. Ruth used to hate the end of the summer but not so much these days. Summers had always meant parties, festivals and long evenings. Maybe it was just her age, but that's not what her summers were like any more. In fact, she had started to love the onset of autumn. It had such a lovely, nostalgic feel to it as a season. The crisp leaves falling, the chance to pull out sweaters and scarves. Long walks in the countryside.

Her train of thought was interrupted by her phone ringing.

It was Nick.

'Hiya. How are you doing?' she asked.

'Fine,' he replied.

'And how's Amanda and my beautiful goddaughter?'

'They're great, although they decided to make bolognese together so our kitchen now resembles a scene from *The Texas Chainsaw Massacre.*'

Ruth laughed. 'At least they're having fun. This a social call?'

'No.' Nick's voice sounded more serious. 'I stopped at Jim's on the way home. I knocked but there was no answer. All the lights were off but his car was on the drive. I shouted through the letterbox, but nothing.'

'Right,' Ruth said, feeling concerned. 'I'm starting to worry now. If we don't hear anything in the morning, I'm going to get uniform to do a forced entry.'

'Yeah. This is all so out of character. I just thought I should let you know.'

'Of course. Thanks, Nick, I'll see you in the morning. Night.'

Ruth ended the call and then looked up at the moon which had just started to appear in the dark sky above her.

'You look deep in thought,' Sarah said as she came over, gave her a kiss, and then handed her a glass of wine.

'Oh, I wasn't going to drink tonight,' Ruth admitted.

Sarah went to take the glass back. 'I'll put it back in the bottle then, shall I?' she asked with an amused grin.

Ruth chortled. 'Don't be insane. You can't hand me a big glass of wine and then take it back.'

Sarah gave her a searching look. 'Everything okay? Who was that on the phone? Work?'

'It was Nick,' Ruth explained, and then looked at her. 'You remember Jim Garrow?'

'Of course. Lovely guy. Bit straight-laced but nice.'

'Yeah, that's him. Or at least it was.'

'What does that mean?'

'We had a murder case over in Wrexham. A mother was killed and eventually we took the daughter to trial over it,' Ruth explained.

Sarah nodded as she sat down opposite Ruth and took

a sip of wine. 'Yes, I remember you telling me about it at the time. And then it was on the local news.'

'Jim was the investigating officer in the case,' Ruth said, 'but he got involved with the daughter.'

Sarah pulled a face. 'Involved?'

'He swore to me that nothing happened between them,' Ruth continued, 'but there was an attraction. However, this woman lied in court, told everyone that they'd slept together. The judge threw the case out.'

Sarah frowned. 'Jesus, I'm surprised Jim's still got a job.'

'He might not have, but it gets worse than that.'

'Worse? Really?' Sarah said incredulously.

'She started to stalk Jim after the trial. She turned up in the garden one night, knocked on the door, stuff like that. Two nights ago, she was hit by a car in the Cross Foxes pub car park. Hit and run.'

'Is she dead?'

'Nearly,' Ruth said. 'She was critical but somehow she's recovered. But she has complete amnesia about the accident. She has no idea who hit her and if it was deliberate.'

'What about Jim?'

'Jim failed to show for work today. And he didn't ring in sick. Nothing.'

Sarah looked at her. 'Where is he?'

'We don't know, but it's incredibly suspicious.'

'You think he ran her down deliberately?'

'I just think it's too much of a coincidence for those two things not to be linked.'

Sarah raised an eyebrow. 'CCTV?'

Ruth shook her head. 'Apparently the Cross Foxes rear car park doesn't have any.'

'So if it was Jim, he's in the clear?'

'Possibly … unless he's done something very stupid which is why he's vanished.'

Sarah gave her a dark look. 'You think he'd take his own life?'

'I don't think so, but after everything that's happened in the past ten days, I'm not sure. Jim is right on the edge.'

Sarah paused and took a long gulp of wine. 'Jesus, your job is never easy, is it?'

'Nope,' Ruth agreed.

Sarah narrowed her eyes. 'And what if you find out that Jim did run her over and drove away?'

'How do you mean?'

'If she has amnesia and there's no CCTV. What do you do if you find out Jim was responsible?'

Ruth shrugged. 'I just don't know.'

'Really?' Sarah asked with an incredulous expression.

'If this was a normal member of the public, I would make him hand himself in immediately. But this woman just isn't a normal member of the public. She's a murdering psychopath.'

'But your job is to uphold the law,' Sarah protested. 'You can't start deciding who it does or doesn't apply to, can you?'

Ruth shrugged, leaned over and stubbed out her cigarette.

'If I'm honest, I have no idea what I'm going to do if that's how it plays out.'

Chapter 16

Georgie marched down the hallway, grabbed her car keys and opened the front door. She had slept well, had a big breakfast, coffee, and was feeling on top of the world. That was one of the perks of being pregnant. As long as she was eating healthily, she could eat as much as she wanted. After all, she was eating for two. And it made up for the first trimester, when she had no appetite and was continually sick. The only strange thing was that she craved pickled food, and in particular pickled beetroot. That and sauerkraut. She had no idea why. She wasn't a huge fan of pickled food in general and she'd only had sauerkraut once on a girls' weekend to Berlin. That was the strange world of pregnancy cravings for you.

As she turned to lock the door, she heard a noise behind her. She knew exactly what it was. Adam returning from his morning bike ride. And obviously she hadn't stalled going into Llancastell nick by fifteen minutes to make sure that she left at the same time as yesterday. <u>And</u> hopefully bumped into Adam again on the way out!

'Morning,' he boomed as he threw his leg from over the saddle and coasted up the drive standing on one pedal.

Neat trick she thought, aware that her pulse had quickened a little.

'Oh hi there,' she said, trying to stifle a silly giggle that seemed to want to escape from her mouth.

Who are you? Pull yourself together, she said to herself.

Adam blew out his cheeks as he unclipped his helmet and took it off. His face was red and shiny. But it only made him more attractive.

The other by-product of being pregnant was an increased libido. In other words, Georgie was feeling very horny. She'd read plenty of articles online that reassured her that this was perfectly normal. But it did add to her attraction to Adam. Essentially she wanted to get him into bed. However, she was a realist. She was pregnant. Adam might not find her attractive. And he might also have a girlfriend or even a wife.

'How far do you go in the mornings?' she asked, keen to keep the conversation flowing.

'Oh, about 40k. Takes me about an hour and a half. It's such a great place to cycle. Especially early in the morning.'

'Yes, it must be,' Georgie said with her best flirty smile, 'although it must annoy your girlfriend when you wake up so early.'

Oh my God, did I actually just say that?

Adam gave her a bemused smile. 'Oh well … Erm, I don't have a girlfriend.'

'Sorry, I don't know why I said that,' Georgie said, pulling a face. 'It's none of my business.'

'It's fine,' Adam reassured her, and then pointed to his house. 'It's just little old me next door.'

There was an awkward silence.

'I was engaged,' he blurted out after a few seconds. 'She cheated on me. So I upped sticks and moved over here. Sort of a new start.'

Could he be any cuter?

'Oh right. I'm sorry to hear that. I mean I'm not sorry you moved in next door. I'm just sorry that your fiancée cheated on you. That sounds horrible.'

Am I gabbling?

'It was,' Adam admitted with a pained expression. 'Actually, I don't think I'm over it yet.'

Georgie gave him an empathetic smile.

'Stupid question,' he said, 'but have you got a drill by any chance? I know that sounds strange but I left mine in Manchester and there's a few odd jobs that need doing now I've moved in.'

Georgie grinned. 'Not a stupid question. And yes, by chance I do have a drill and all the drill bits to go with it.'

Adam looked directly at her and gave her a flirty smile. 'Well, check you out!'

'I hope to be home just after 6pm. Obviously that might all change but I can bring it round.'

'Perfect,' he said. 'I look forward to that.'

'Great, I'll see you later.' Georgie walked away and reminded herself not to do a little dance or jump up and click her heels as she went.

Chapter 17

'Okay everyone,' Ruth said as she strode across the CID office towards a scene board that had been set up. Although there had been no confirmation that the body in the back of the car was indeed Martin Jones, there was still a photo of him in the middle of the board. He was wearing a red Welsh rugby shirt and was holding up a pint of beer to whoever had taken the photo. There were also small photos of Andy Fletcher, the man who had died in the crane accident at the Heswall site, and his wife Sonia Fletcher. His accident felt like it might be relevant if it was Martin who had been murdered. There was also a large map of The Wirral with a red pin marking where in Heswall the Headline Properties development site was located. The Wirral Peninsular, to give it its technical name, was seven miles wide and eleven miles long. It was separated from the Welsh mainland to the west by the Dee Estuary, and to the east, the Merseyside Estuary. In Old English, The Wirral translated as *Myrtle Corner*. Myrtle was a plant mainly found in marshes and bogs but it was no longer found in the area. The first settlements on The

Wirral dated back to 12,000 BC in Greasby, Irby and Hoylake.

'Let's get up to speed,' Ruth said as she looked out at the assembled CID team.

Nick came into the office with a sense of urgency and looked over. 'Boss, DNA results have come back. The body in the back of the car is Martin Jones.'

It wasn't a big surprise, and it did mean that they could now focus on Martin as being their victim. It would be devastating news for all of Martin Jones' family. For a moment, Ruth thought of Martin's three children, all of whom were under the age of ten. It was tragic.

'Right, well that is what we suspected,' she said quietly as she pointed to a photograph of him on the board. 'This is now our confirmed victim. Martin Jones. Let's just recap what we do know. Aged thirty seven. He lives in Wrexham with his wife Steph. Three children. Martin co-owned a successful building company, Headline Properties. He was found on the back seat of his burned out car. He had received several severe blows to the side of his skull,' Ruth explained, and then she pointed to a map of The Wirral. 'But the murder happened in Heswall. That means we are going to be liaising with Merseyside Police on this.'

There were a few groans.

Ruth gave the team a knowing look. 'I know. I know. The last time we worked with a police force from across the border it didn't go very well. Bloody English, eh?'

The team laughed at her ironic joke. The joint investigation with the police in Chester had been very problematic.

'My first impression of Detective Inspector Gorski yesterday is that she is a team player, so I'm going to be optimistic about this,' she said. 'Nick?'

'I agree. DI Gorski seemed to be above board.' Nick

came over, perched himself on the table and looked at the team. 'Okay. Martin Jones told his wife that he was going to the gym early yesterday morning before going into work at the offices in Wrexham. We've checked with the gym. He was never there. Steph Jones also told us that he went to the gym every morning like clockwork at around 6 to 6.30am. According to Total Fitness gym, he hadn't been there for three months. So where had he been going every morning? And we've also checked with Headline Properties. He didn't have an appointment at the site at Heswall yesterday morning.'

Ruth nodded. 'So, why did Martin keep lying about where he was going? And what was he doing in Heswall early yesterday morning? Let's contact traffic. See if we can get a visual or an ANPR hit on his car yesterday. Did he leave home and go straight to Heswall or did he stop en route? I want us to liaise with the CID officers in Heswall. I want to know if there are any CCTV cameras at that site. I'm sure they're checking that right now. I need us to pull Martin's phone records. Find out every call he made or received in the 48 hours before his murder for starters. And then work back from there. Get hold of his bank statements, emails and social media. And can we check the death of Andy Fletcher? It feels significant. As far as I can see, the only people who had a strong motive to kill Martin were Andy Fletcher's wife Sonia or possibly other members of his family. See if we can check their whereabouts yesterday.'

Kennedy looked over at Ruth. 'Boss, Professor Amis would like to see you over at the preliminary post-mortem. He's got a couple of things he'd like to show you.'

Ruth rolled her eyes. 'He always does.'

Nick gave a wry smile. 'At least he doesn't annoy you, eh?' he said sardonically.

Georgie approached and looked at Ruth. 'Boss, can I have a quick word?' She gestured towards Ruth's office to imply that she would like to have a word in private.

As they went into her office, Ruth gave her a concerned look. She and Georgie had become very close in recent months, especially as Georgie was dealing with being pregnant on her own. If she was honest, Ruth was also angry with Georgie's parents who seemed to show virtually no interest in the fact that they would soon have their first grandchild. It didn't make any sense to Ruth. Why the hell weren't they excited by that?

'Everything okay?' she asked in a worried tone.

'Oh it's not me. I'm fine,' Georgie reassured her, and then pulled a face. 'It's Jim. I spoke to him a couple of minutes before you came in for briefing. He said that he has terrible stomach flu which is why he hasn't been in. And he apologised for going AWOL yesterday.'

Ruth sighed. 'Yeah, well I'm not impressed. How did he sound?'

'He sounded terrible,' Georgie said, frowning. 'Actually, he sounded drunk, boss.'

Chapter 18

Ruth pushed through the double doors into the Llancastell University Hospital mortuary, followed by Nick. The air was thick with the smell of preserving chemicals and detergents, and the temperature dropped to a ghostly chill. Her concerns about Garrow, his whereabouts, and his involvement in Lucy Morgan's hit and run were growing. She and Nick would need to go to his home at some point and confront him.

Ruth looked around at the mortuary examination tables, gurneys, aluminium trays, workbenches, and an assortment of luminous chemicals. Then she spotted the burned corpse on the far side of the room. Chief Pathologist, Professor Tony Amis, was taking photographs, using a small white plastic ruler to give an indication of scale. Attached to his pastel blue scrubs was a small microphone, as post-mortems were all now digitally recorded.

'This was a bit of a grisly surprise today,' he said, gesturing to Martin Jones' body as he approached. 'Almost put me off my lunch.'

Nick rolled his eyes. 'Almost?'

'Well, my wife had got me in some lovely ox tongue from our local butchers. And she'd made me tongue, tomato and mustard sandwiches with thick cut white bread and butter,' Amis explained, and then kissed his fingers to show how delicious the sandwich was. 'I don't think anything would have put me off eating that.'

Jesus, Ruth thought as she shuddered. The terrible condition of Martin's burned body and Amis' wittering about his sandwich made her feel sick. She gave him a withering look and then spotted his latest mug. It had a slogan on it – *Yes, I am a doctor. And no, I don't want to look at it, thanks!*

Ruth and Nick shared a look of resigned disbelief.

'Have you found the cause of death yet?' Ruth asked. Even though she had seen burned bodies before, Martin's was particularly bad. His limbs were black, red and twisted. She turned away, making a mental note not to look again if she could help it.

Amis went over to a couple of x-rays that were pinned to a light box on the wall. 'Well, your victim received six severe blows to the head,' he said as he pointed. 'Blunt force trauma. This one here fractured the skull. My guess would be that he was hit with something metallic, but I can't be sure. These indentations in the skull are unusual.'

Ruth raised an eyebrow. 'Unusual? How do you mean?'

'Well,' Amis went closer to the x-rays and touched his forefinger against one of them. 'You see here? The indentations are exactly five inches long. And the weapon has left a very distinctive, regular wound. I can rule out a hammer or something like that. And if your victim had been attacked with a baseball bat or an iron bar, the wounds would have been far less precise.' Then Amis looked at them. 'To be honest, I'm a bit stumped as to what he was attacked with.'

'Right,' Ruth said. 'Anything else?'

'Forensics have confirmed that the fire in the car was started deliberately.'

'Which is no big surprise,' Nick added.

'No,' Amis agreed. 'They have discovered traces of an accelerant. Possibly petrol, but they haven't confirmed that yet. Chemical analysis will tell us more. And we also found some form of clothing in the back of the car that was separate to the victim's clothing. It was badly damaged, but forensics are having a look.'

'So, Martin Jones was killed before he was moved into the car?' Nick asked.

'No.' Amis pulled a face. 'Despite the blows to his skull, the actual cause of death was asphyxiation.'

Ruth frowned. 'He was strangled?'

Amis shook his head. 'No, sorry. Your victim was still alive when he was put into the car. He might have been semi-conscious, but he actually died from smoke inhalation.'

'Okay,' Ruth said as she processed this information. Then she looked at Amis. 'Let me know if there's anything else once you've completed the post-mortem.'

'Of course.'

Ruth and Nick turned to leave. But then Ruth thought of something.

'Actually Tony,' Ruth said as she turned back to face him. 'There is something else. I need a favour from you.'

'Hey, anything for my favourite female detective inspector in the whole world,' he said theatrically.

A smile tugged at Ruth's lips. 'How many female DIs do you actually know, Tony?'

Amis chortled. 'Well, yes. There is only you, but just ask away.'

'There was an accident over at a building site in

Heswall on The Wirral last year. April 2020 I believe. A workman, Andy Fletcher, fell from a high crane and was killed. Could you have a quick look and see if you can dig out his post-mortem?'

'Okay, I think that would have been carried out at the Arrowe Park Hospital.'

'Could you give the PM a once-over and see if there's anything unusual in there?'

Amis narrowed his eyes. 'What exactly am I looking for?'

'I don't actually know,' Ruth admitted. 'It might be that he was fit and healthy and just the poor victim of an accident. But I'd just like to check to see if there were any anomalies.'

'No problem. I'll take a look,' he replied.

Chapter 19

Ruth and Nick were now sitting in a meeting room opposite Gorski on the ground floor of Bebington nick. It was an ugly concrete block of a building that looked like it belonged in Eastern Europe rather than the leafy suburbs of The Wirral. They had brought Gorski up to speed with what they had found out so far.

Gorski leaned forward and opened a file that was in front of her. Ruth noticed that her nails were very well manicured, and she wore a small diamond ring on her left hand.

'We've pulled some of Martin Jones' social media,' she explained and then looked over. 'You mentioned this accident in which Andy Fletcher died last year on the site in Heswall.'

Ruth nodded. 'Martin's wife and sister seemed to think that Andy Fletcher's widow Sonia held Martin accountable for his death.'

Gorski raised an eyebrow knowingly. 'You could say that,' she said sardonically. 'Sonia Fletcher has waged a one-woman war against Martin Jones ever since the accident. She's written to her local MP demanding a full enquiry. And there's been some very unpleasant stuff written on social media. Some of it from Sonia and some of it from some of Andy's friends and family.'

'Anything we should be worried about?' Nick asked.

Gorski nodded as she pulled out a printout. 'This account is very active. *@mattthelad'79.* Last week was the one-year anniversary of the accident. There was a post on this account saying that Martin Jones was '… a coward and lying scumbag who deserves to die for what happened to Andy.' There are some others who chip in saying 'I'll help you mate'.'

Ruth raised an eyebrow. 'Any idea about who the addresses belong to?'

Gorski shook her head. 'We've asked the media company for details and IP addresses, but you know how long that can take. Sonia Fletcher lives over in Buckley, so if you can, go and have a word.'

Nick nodded. 'No problem.'

Ruth's phone rang. She looked at the number and saw that it was Professor Amis.

'Sorry, but I need to take this,' she said as she got up and walked over to the corner of the room while Nick and Gorski continued to talk.

'Tony,' Ruth said as she answered her phone.

'I'm sitting looking at that post-mortem on Andrew Fletcher from April 2020,' he said. 'They've just emailed it over to me from the Coroner's Office.'

'Anything of interest?' Ruth asked.

'Actually, there is. I've got the toxicology report. Andrew Fletcher's blood alcohol level was 1.0% at the time of his death.'

Ruth had a vague idea and certainly knew that this was over the drink driving limit. 'How many units is that?'

'At a guess, five or six units.'

'And what time did they pronounce him dead?'

'According to the death certificate, 11.28am. He died at the scene … the fall broke his neck.'

'So effectively he was drunk when he was on that crane?'

'Yes,' Amis agreed, 'plus there are traces of benzodiazepine in his blood.'

'Valium?'

'Precisely. The mixture of that and alcohol is pretty potent. And he certainly shouldn't have been up a crane doing any kind of work in that state.'

Ruth frowned. 'Didn't this all come out in the investigation?'

'Yes. The Health and Safety Executive did a full investigation,' Amis explained. 'His death was ruled as accidental with mitigating circumstances.'

'Right. That's interesting and thank you for turning that around so quickly.'

'Anything for you, Ruth,' Amis said, sounding a little smarmy.

'Bye Tony,' Ruth said, ending the call.

'Anything interesting?' Nick asked as she came back to the table.

Ruth raised an eyebrow. 'I don't know if it helps us or if it's relevant, but Andy Fletcher was drunk and had taken Valium when he fell off that crane last April.'

Chapter 20

Ruth and Nick had just sat down with Steph and Lilly in the living room of the Jones' home again. It had been an hour since Kennedy had broken the news to them that the DNA showed that it had been Martin in the car.

Georgie sat quietly on a chair over by the door.

'I'm so sorry for your loss,' Ruth said gently. 'Do you think you'd be up to a few questions at the moment?'

Lilly reached across to Steph, held her hand and looked at her. 'Is that okay?' she asked in a virtual whisper.

Steph looked at her and nodded almost imperceptibly.

Ruth wasn't sure if it was her imagination, but there seemed to be an intimacy between Lilly and Steph that was unusual between a sister-in-law and wife. Was there something in that, she wondered? She wasn't sure.

Steph sniffed and wiped her tear-streaked face with a tissue.

Nick pulled out his notebook and pen. 'Did Martin say anything about where he was going after he'd been to the gym?'

Steph shook her head and then shrugged. 'I just assumed that he was going into the office.'

'The Headline Properties office in Wrexham?' Nick asked to clarify.

'Yes,' Steph said, and then frowned. 'Did you speak to anyone at the gym?'

'Yes.' Ruth took a moment. 'I'm afraid Martin didn't go to the gym yesterday morning. He hasn't been there for a couple of months.'

'What? No, that's not true. He told me …' Steph stopped and looked utterly bewildered. 'But Martin goes there every morning before he goes to the office. I saw him pack up his stuff. I don't understand.'

Nick looked over. 'Was there anything troubling Martin in recent weeks? Or was there anything unusual or out of the ordinary that had happened?'

Lilly and Steph looked at each other.

'No,' Lilly replied. 'As far as I know, everything was normal.'

Ruth narrowed her eyes. 'Were you very close to your brother?'

Lilly nodded and looked upset. 'Yes. We were very close. Our mother died when we were young, and our dad wasn't around much. We just had each other a lot of the time.'

'And the accident involving Andy Fletcher …' Ruth said, '… did Martin say anything about it recently?'

'No.' Steph looked puzzled. 'As far as I knew, there had been an industrial tribunal and police investigation. And it was just a terrible accident.'

Nick arched his brows. 'Martin didn't mention that he'd been attacked on social media. Or that Sonia Fletcher had been to her MP to demand that her husband's death be looked at again?'

Steph and Lilly looked at each other in confusion.

'No,' Lilly replied. 'I thought that it had all been dealt with. I had no idea any of that was going on.'

Steph nodded in agreement. 'No. Martin never mentioned any of that.'

Ruth sat forward. 'And there's no one else that you can think of who would want to harm your husband?'

'No. Do you think Sonia Fletcher had something to do with this?'

'We don't know at the moment,' Ruth admitted as she got up from where she was sitting. 'Okay. We're going to go now but we will obviously keep you informed of any developments.'

'Thank you,' Lilly said.

Ruth and Nick went out through the door and into the hallway with Georgie.

They approached the front door and Ruth beckoned Georgie to follow them outside.

'What do you make of Steph and Lilly's relationship?' Ruth asked her.

Georgie gave her a quizzical frown. 'How do you mean?'

'They're very close, aren't they?' Ruth said in way that implied that there was subtext to her question.

Georgie cottoned on to what Ruth might be implying. 'You mean are they close, or are they close?'

Nick shrugged and looked at Ruth. 'Well, if your gaydar is receiving a signal, then we should probably do some digging.'

'I know what you mean,' Georgie agreed. 'Steph is very needy, and Lilly seems to take care of her. It definitely struck me as a bit weird given they are sister-in-law and wife.'

Ruth stifled a sigh. 'Okay. Well keep an eye on that while you're here, would you?'

'Yes, boss,' Georgie replied.

Chapter 21

Ruth had called Garrow several times during the day but hadn't heard anything back. She and Nick had decided to go via his home on the way back to Llancastell nick. The news of Lucy Morgan's accident had weighed heavily at the back of Ruth's mind all day. Garrow's failure to show up for work, his flimsy excuse, and Georgie's comment that she thought he sounded drunk on the phone all rang alarm bells.

Garrow's home was a small, detached house in a cul-de-sac of new builds. They pulled up outside and got out. The sun was beginning to set and the air was colder than it had been all day.

'His car isn't here,' Nick observed as they walked up the garden path to Garrow's front door.

'I hope he's not bloody driving,' Ruth grumbled.

Nick gave the door a heavy knock and stood back.

The garden was immaculate. Neat lawn, small rockery, and then a few well-placed plants and bushes. Garrow had 'a quality' that had made Ruth wonder about his sexuality on several occasions. There was nothing soft about him.

She'd seen him handle himself well in the most frightening situations. And he wasn't camp. But there were moments when she caught just a phrase or gesture. However, his tryst with Lucy Morgan had shown that he was definitely interested in women. Maybe he was bisexual. Frankly it was none of her business, and maybe the very fact that she even thought about it showed what a dinosaur she was. She was pretty sure that the millennial or even Gen Z officers didn't give things like that a second thought. Someone's sexuality these days seemed irrelevant, unimportant, and fluid in its nature. And Ruth had to admit it was a vast improvement on when she had first come out in the 90s.

Nick knocked again.

Nothing.

'Bloody hell,' Ruth said with a sigh. Then she turned and looked at the empty drive. 'Where the hell is he?'

While Nick crouched down to look through the letterbox, Ruth went over to the ground floor window. Even though the curtains were pulled, she cupped her hands to look inside.

All she could see was the living room in darkness, the carpet, and the edge of Garrow's sofa. There was nothing to give any clue as to if he was inside or not.

'Jim?' Nick shouted through the letterbox. 'Jim? It's Nick.'

Ruth came back over as Nick stood up.

She became aware of a noise and looked over at a neighbour – late 60s, male, balding with glasses - who was watering his hanging baskets with a watering can. He was giving Ruth and Nick a very suspicious look, and it was clear that he was using the excuse of watering his flowers to keep an eye on what they were up to.

Taking out her warrant card, Ruth walked across

Garrow's lawn, over the gravel and into the neighbour's garden.

'Evening,' she said with a friendly expression. 'I'm wondering if you know Jim who lives next door?'

The neighbour put the watering can down and came over to look at her warrant card as if he wanted to check that it wasn't fake.

Ruth shot a curious look at Nick. She couldn't remember the last time a member of the public had inspected her ID. In fact, she wasn't sure that anyone ever had.

Bloody cheek.

'Detective Inspector Hunter. And that's Detective Sergeant Evans. We're from Llancastell CID,' she explained with hidden amusement. 'We're work colleagues of Jim's. We assume that you know he is a police officer?'

'Oh yes. Of course,' he replied enthusiastically. 'Bit of a bonus having a detective living next door to us. You know, with security and crime what it is these days.'

Is he having a pop at me? Ruth wondered.

'Have you seen him lately?' Nick asked as he wandered over.

'Yes. Sorry, I should have said. He went out about half an hour ago.'

'Right. Thank you. I don't suppose he said where he was going by any chance?'

'No, but he had been taking some cuttings from his garden, so he had a bunch of flowers in his hand when he got in the car.'

Ruth gave Nick a puzzled look. *What was that about?*

The neighbour moved forward to indicate that he wanted to talk quietly and possibly divulge something sensitive.

'Look, I'm not sure if I should tell you this but Jim's

eyes were bloodshot,' he muttered under his breath. 'I think he'd been drinking.'

Ruth gave him a forced smile. 'Okay. Thank you for telling us. And thanks for your help.'

'I don't want Jim to get into any trouble. He's such a lovely young man,' he remarked as he picked up his watering can.

Ruth and Nick made their way back to their car.

Nick frowned at her. 'Flowers? Where's he going with flowers? He can't possibly be meeting a woman.'

Ruth gave him a knowing look. 'I know exactly where he's gone.'

Chapter 22

Georgie was sitting outside in the back garden at the Jones' home. She knew that Ruth had given her the 'cushy' job of family liaison officer as a way of keeping her safe while she was pregnant. Even though Georgie didn't necessarily want to have special treatment or favouritism, it wasn't that long ago that she had been kidnapped while in the line of duty. And now she had a new life inside of her, it seemed selfish to put herself in danger when she didn't need to.

Her mind then turned to her new neighbour Adam as she glanced down at her phone. It was 6.30pm and she'd told him that she'd be home just after 6pm. As far as she knew, there had been no more significant developments in the investigation that day. Ruth would have called her if there had been. And Steph had made it clear that she didn't want or need her to stay over.

However, Georgie remembered being given the job of family liaison officer when she was in uniform and relatively new on the job. A 16-year-old boy, Scott, had been stabbed and killed outside his school in rural Snowdonia. His single mother, Kathy, had gone completely to pieces.

Scott was her only child. Scott's father had died seven years earlier from cancer. Kathy just needed constant reassurance and support as the investigation proceeded. Georgie found herself sleeping on the sofa at the family home most nights after talking Kathy 'off the ledge' often into the early hours. Georgie didn't mind. She could see how much Kathy was struggling with the death of her son. Eventually, a 15-year-old boy was convicted of Scott's murder and sentenced to 23 years. And Georgie had to leave and let Kathy try to rebuild her life.

Georgie sat back, took a long deep breath and thought she would leave for the night in about five minutes. She looked at the neat garden. The amber of the setting sun was dappling through the leaves of the overhanging trees which shook in the breeze and threw a speckled pattern across the lawn. At the far end of the garden, a neighbour's catalpa tree, with its huge spherical leaves, loped casually over their wall. Over to the left, there was a small path of rose-coloured bricks and a wooden archway. Against the wall was a flowerbed that needed tending as it had white flowering nettles, and willowherbs and moss were growing on the lower bricks of the garden wall.

The air was thick with a sort of powdery smell. Georgie wondered if it was the moss or maybe the flowers of the nettles. As she moved her chair back, a cuckoo started its rhythmic call in the distance. There was something about the repetition of the noise – its urgency, precision, reprise – that she found slightly unnerving. As if the cuckoo was warning of something that she wasn't aware of.

'You off soon?' Lilly asked in a quiet voice.

Georgie turned to look at her. With her tresses of brunette hair falling on her shoulder, pale alabaster skin, and cerulean, blue eyes, Lilly looked like a woman from a pre-Raphaelite painting that Georgie had studied when she took A-level art. Rossetti was the name of one of the artists, if she remembered correctly.

'Yes, unless there's something that you or Steph would like to talk about?'

'No.' Lilly shook her head sadly. 'It just feels like I'm in some terrible dream and I'm going to wake up and it won't be true. And Martin will be alive.' Lilly looked at her. 'Does that sound strange?'

'No, not at all,' Georgie reassured her. 'I lost someone a few months ago. Sometimes I'd wake and for a few seconds I would completely forget that they were gone. And then it would come flooding back, and it was just so painful.'

'I'm sorry to hear that,' Lilly said in an empathetic tone as she and Georgie walked back towards the kitchen. 'Do you think that it has something to do with this accident that happened last year?'

Georgie shrugged as they went inside. 'I'm sorry. We just don't know at the moment. And it's not really for me to speculate.'

'No of course,' Lilly said as they walked down the hallway towards the front door.

'Tell Steph that I said goodbye and that I'll see you guys in the morning.'

'I might come over a bit later tomorrow,' Lilly said as she opened the front door and Georgie went down the steps.

'Okay, well I'll see you at some point.'

Lilly smiled and then closed the door.

Georgie walked down the drive towards her car which was parked out on the road.

Then she turned back to look at the house.

She spotted Lilly through the window walking into the living room.

Steph came over and they embraced.

And then the two women kissed passionately.

Georgie took a double take. *What the …?*

The kiss and embrace became increasingly passionate.

Okay, I didn't expect to see that, Georgie thought to herself even though Ruth had flagged up her suspicions.

Chapter 23

Ruth and Nick arrived at St Mary's Church and graveyard to the west of Llancastell. On the way over there, Ruth had told Nick that she suspected that Garrow had gone to see Detective Sergeant Dan French's grave. French had been Garrow's partner and friend. He had died in the line of duty only last week, and Ruth knew that the combination of French's sudden death, and the mistrial and encounters with Lucy Morgan had sent him Garrow off the rails. She didn't blame him. It would have been too much for anyone to have to deal with.

Making their way through the graves, their feet crunched noisily on the twisting gravel pathway. Dark green lichens covered many of the older gravestones that flanked the path. Ruth noticed how the headstones were all different shapes and sizes. The lettering on them had been worn away by the wind, rain, and time itself, so that many of the letters were now illegible under their thick layers of moss.

Up ahead was a huge, towering monument of a tomb that resembled an altar, with deep indentations marking out rows of names. Its granite face was carved into grooves with seaweed-like tufts of lichen creeping outwards from the seams. Huge flowers wrapped around the base like climbing vines and extended upwards towards the sky.

In the distance, Ruth spotted a forlorn figure sitting by a freshly dug grave.

'How did you know he'd be here?' Nick asked.

Ruth shrugged. 'I know Dan's death has knocked Jim for six. He had flowers. It was an educated guess.'

As they made their way down the gravel path, the late summer air was heavy with a sweet aroma. The sky above was now a darkening blue and even though it wasn't dark yet, stars were beginning to appear.

Garrow was sitting hugging his knees looking at the grave. There was a half empty bottle of Jack Daniel's laying on the grass beside him.

'Hello Jim,' Ruth said gently.

Looking startled, Garrow looked up at them. He was fairly drunk and had been crying.

'I've been talking to Dan,' he explained as he gestured to the freshly dug earth where several bunches of flowers had been laid, along with some battery-powered candles and cards of condolence.

'Are you okay?' Nick asked.

Garrow pointed to the grave. 'You see I wanted to ask his advice. He was always very good at giving me advice. Very wise.'

'Yes, he was,' Ruth agreed.

'Sounds stupid, doesn't it,' Garrow said with a half laugh, 'coming here to ask him what I should do?'

'No, it doesn't sound stupid at all,' Ruth reassured him. 'I miss Dan very much too.'

Nick went over to the bottle of Jack Daniel's and picked it up from the grass. Then he looked down at

Garrow. 'Trust me, mate. Drinking the rest of this isn't going to make you feel any better. And in the morning, you're going to feel a million times worse. I should know.'

Garrow looked broken, and nodded his head as if he was defeated.

Nick unscrewed the top of the bottle and poured the whiskey away.

'Why don't you come with us, Jim?' Ruth suggested in a quiet voice.

'I can't.' He looked up at her and shook his head. 'A couple of weeks ago, my life was so perfect. I just didn't realise it. But it was.' His words were a little slurry. 'And now it's all gone. Just like that.' He clicked his fingers.

'We can drive you home, Jim,' Nick suggested, 'and you can tell us what's been going on.'

'What's been going on?' Garrow gave an ironic snort. 'I'll tell you what's been going on.' He moved his hands in a dramatic gesture. 'She's gone. Lucy Morgan is no more. She's dead. Finished. Did you know that? And I killed her.'

Ruth crouched down and looked directly in his eyes. 'No you didn't,' she said gently. 'She's not dead, Jim.'

'What?' Garrow sneered as he tried to get up.

Nick helped him to his feet. 'Here we go, mate.'

For a few seconds, Garrow steadied himself and brushed the earth off his trousers.

Then he looked at them both.

'Yes she is,' he said in a slurred voice. 'I bloody killed her. Stupid bitch stood in front of my car. I'd had enough so I drove at her and I killed her.'

Ruth moved closer to him and put her hand on his arm. 'Well, Nick and I visited her in hospital last night. She received a nasty bump to the head but by some twist of fate she's very much alive, Jim.'

Garrow looked doubtful and swallowed hard. 'Really?'

Nick nodded. 'Yes, mate, really.'

'What did she say to you?' he asked.

'She said that she remembers going to the Cross Foxes pub,' Ruth explained, but she has no recollection of the accident or what happened. Nothing. She has amnesia.'

'How long for?'

'We have no idea. It might be temporary, but if we're very lucky, the accident will have been permanently eradicated from her memory. I've seen it lots of times before.'

Garrow shook his head in disbelief. 'She doesn't remember anything?' he said under his breath as if he couldn't quite believe it.

'Come on,' Ruth said as moved her hand to his shoulder. 'You're in no fit state to drive anywhere so we'll drop you home.'

Garrow nodded as they began to walk back through the graveyard towards the car park. Then he shook his head again. 'I really thought she was dead. I really thought I'd killed her.'

'We know you did,' Ruth said as they got to the gates.

Chapter 24

Georgie looked in the mirror in the hallway of her home. She'd reapplied her lipstick and touched up her makeup twice. She peered closely at her reflection.

God, I look tired. I thought pregnancy was meant to make you radiant?

Putting her hand through her hair, she moved it back off her face. Then she rejigged her jacket and her blouse. Then she caught herself and had a reality check.

You are aware that you're pregnant, aren't you? she said to herself in a withering tone.

But there was another part of her that was ignoring the sensible part of her mind. Chatting to Adam was the most exciting thing that had happened to her in weeks. She didn't want boring old rational logic to ruin her buzz.

Right, here we go, she thought as she took the chewing gum out of her mouth, plopped it in the bin in the hall, opened the front door, went outside, and closed the front door.

Then she stopped.

The drill, you moron! Placenta brain!

Opening the front door again, she grabbed the drill box by its dark blue handle, locked the door, and proceeded to walk around to Adam's house. It had occurred to her that he might just open the door, take the drill, thank her and then say goodbye and close the door. In fact, that's probably what he was going to do.

She knocked on the door and took a step back.

A few seconds later, the door opened and Adam peered out. So far, she'd only seen him red and sweaty after his morning bike ride.

Now wearing a navy hoodie, grey joggers and slides, he looked even better.

'One drill, as requested,' she said in a chirpy voice as she held the drill box aloft.

'Great,' he said with a smile. Then he gestured. 'Do you want to come in?'

Yes!

'Erm, why not,' she said, pretending to be in two minds.

'You'll have to excuse the mess,' he said apologetically. 'I'm still living out of boxes at the moment.'

Georgie went inside and Adam closed the door behind them.

Chapter 25

Having taken Garrow home and made sure that he got into the house safely, Ruth and Nick were now sitting outside his house in their car.

Ruth took a long drag from her cigarette and buzzed down the window.

Nick glanced at her. 'You think he's going to be all right?'

'I hope so,' she sighed as she blew smoke out of the window. 'He really has fucked things up.'

'Dare I ask what we're going to do about it?' Nick asked with a concerned look.

Ruth took another drag and shook her head. 'You mean we have a fellow officer who tried to run down someone and kill them?'

'Yeah. That about sums it up, although there might be some who would argue that Lucy Morgan hasn't suffered any lasting injuries.'

Ruth thought about what Nick had said. 'Isn't the law about intent? If Jim intended to kill her, is it okay if we look the other way?'

Nick shrugged. 'Listen, if she had been an innocent member of the general public, then I'd have no hesitation in handing Jim in. But there are very serious mitigating circumstances here.'

Ruth raised an eyebrow. 'It's not our job to look at the mitigating circumstances. Did Jim break the law? Yes. Did he attempt to kill someone by driving at them when he was drunk? Yes.'

There were a few seconds of silence.

'You really think we should arrest him?' Nick asked with a quizzical expression.

Ruth sighed. 'No, I don't. I'm just playing devil's advocate. And it's not up to us to bend the law or turn a blind eye when it's one of our own who's guilty.'

Nick narrowed his eyes. 'But?'

'But we know that Lucy Morgan brutally murdered her mother in cold blood and then faked amnesia to mislead the investigation. She manipulated Jim and lied in court so that not only were the charges dropped against her, but Jim now faces losing his career as a police officer. And since then, she has effectively stalked and harassed him, causing him psychological torment.' Ruth paused for a moment and glanced sideways at Nick. 'So, should the law protect someone like that? No. And should an officer like Jim go to prison for his reaction to all that? No.'

'Okay,' Nick said, sounding relieved. 'I'm glad we see it like that.'

'It doesn't sit well with me, mind you,' Ruth admitted.

'No, nor me,' Nick agreed, 'but Jim sitting in prison when Lucy Morgan is walking around doesn't feel right either.'

'No.'

There were a few seconds of thoughtful silence before Nick started the engine and they pulled away.

Chapter 26

'Morning everyone,' Ruth said as she strode across the CID office. 'If we can get going please.' Arriving at the scene board, she took a sip from her lukewarm coffee and then looked out at the team. 'Right, what have we got?'

Georgie raised her hand. Even though she was acting as the FLO for Steph Jones, she clocked in for briefing every morning.

'Boss,' she said. 'You were right with your suspicions about Steph Jones and Lilly. When I left the house yesterday evening, I just happened to glance back. I saw them kissing. And I mean really <u>kissing</u>.'

Ruth raised a doubtful brow. 'You sure they weren't just upset or consoling each other?'

'Oh no, boss,' Georgie said, widening her eyes. 'There was no mistaking what was going on.'

Ruth nodded as she processed this information. 'Steph Jones was having an affair with her husband's sister behind his back. Unless this has only just happened?'

Georgie shook her head. 'I think that's unlikely.

They're both grieving so I can't see this happening for the first time right now given the circumstances.'

'No, that's a good point,' Ruth agreed. 'Do we think that they're somehow involved in Martin's murder?'

Georgie furrowed her brow. 'I can't see it. I know we only have Lilly's word for it, but it does seem that she and Martin were close. And I don't suppose that either of them is about to come clean to us that they're having some kind of relationship.'

'Okay, see if you can broach the subject tactfully,' Ruth suggested.

'Yes, boss. I'll do my best.'

'Thanks Georgie.'

Ruth quickly cast an eye over the team. 'What about forensics on the car?'

Nick shook his head. 'The fire destroyed virtually any chance of finding anything useful I'm afraid boss. But they have found some trace DNA on the sole of one of Martin's shoes. It's going to be difficult to get a match but they're going to give it their best shot. But in the words of the chief forensics officer, *don't hold your breath.*'

'Yeah, I was afraid of that.' Ruth pulled a frustrated face. 'Martin's phone records?'

'Still waiting,' Kennedy said.

'Anyone got anything else so far?'

Kennedy indicated that she wanted to speak. 'Yeah, there is something I wanted to show everyone.'

'Thank God for that,' Ruth said. 'I thought we'd ground to a halt before we'd even got started.'

Kennedy went over to her laptop, clicked a button, and activated the large monitor that was mounted to the wall of the CID office. 'We got Martin's bank records over. I checked and he went to the Esso Service Station over towards Neston at 6.29am on the day he was killed and filled up his car with petrol.'

Nick gave a dark look. 'Which is why the fire was so intense. Full petrol tank.'

'Sounds about right,' Ruth agreed.

Kennedy clicked another button and CCTV footage of a petrol station appeared on the monitor. 'I got the CCTV video from the Esso garage sent over to have a look at. I wanted to check that it was Martin who put the petrol in his car, and to see if there was anyone in the car with him.'

Ruth raised a quizzical eyebrow. 'Anything useful?'

Since arriving in Llancastell CID, Kennedy had shown herself to be a very resourceful, sharp detective and a huge asset to the team.

'Not what I expected,' Kennedy admitted as she played the footage. It showed Martin Jones pulling up to a petrol pump, getting out, and then starting to fill his car with petrol. 'As you can see, Martin pulls up and he is on his own. I thought there was nothing else, but then watch this.'

The footage shows another car pull up alongside to an adjacent pump. A woman gets out of a small van and goes to the pump, but then clearly spots and recognises Martin.

The woman storms over and, even though there is no audio, it's clear that she is shouting at Martin who is taken aback by her sudden appearance. Then she slaps him across the face before marching back over to her van and driving away.

'Bloody hell,' Nick said as his eyes widened. 'What's all that about?'

Martin, who now looks shocked, takes the pump out of his car, rubs his face, and then goes inside to pay before driving away.

'Have we any idea who that is?' Ruth asked Kennedy.

'Yes, boss. I ran the plates through the DVLA. The car is registered to Sonia Fletcher. Andy Fletcher's wife.'

'So, she assaulted Martin just before he was murdered. And she was in the area at the right time,' Ruth said as she thought out loud. 'Looks like having a little chat with Sonia Fletcher is now top of our priority list.'

Chapter 27

Ruth and Nick pulled up outside a small tiling, carpet, and flooring shop on the Wrexham Industrial Estate. The name above the shop read *Jarett's* in bright red letters.

Getting out of the car, Nick gestured to a small white van that was parked over to the side of the shop. 'Looks like Sonia Fletcher's van that was on the CCTV.'

Ruth nodded in agreement as they walked up the pavement and up to the door of the shop.

Pushing the glass door open, Ruth was immediately hit by the strong, thick smell of carpets in the shop. There were stacks of carpet samples, along with rugs and other samples up on the walls. On the far side, there was a tiling section with a long display of kitchen and bathroom tiles in all sorts of colours and styles.

Behind a table sat a young man – 30s, smart clothes, slightly gormless face – who looked at them as they approached.

'Morning,' he said as he sat upright in his office chair. 'How can I help?'

Don't get excited, sunshine, we're not here to buy carpets, Ruth thought dryly.

Ruth and Nick fished out their warrant cards to show him.

'DI Hunter and DS Evans, Llancastell CID,' Ruth explained. 'We're looking for Sonia Fletcher?'

The young man's face had fallen with the sight of their warrant cards. 'Oh right,' he said, sounding flustered. 'Erm, she should be out the back in our warehouse.' Then he pointed to a black door marked with a green *Exit* sign. 'You can get out to the back through there if you want?'

Ruth gave him a half smile. 'Thanks for your help.'

They walked over to the door, opened it, and went outside.

There was a concrete loading bay, a couple of large Luton vans, and a huge warehouse in front of them.

One of the vans had its back open and two men were loading long, heavy rolls of carpet. Another van had its engine running, filling the air with the smell of diesel. A radio played the chatter from *TalkSPORT* from somewhere nearby.

The men carrying the carpet stopped as Ruth and Nick approached.

'Don't mind us lads,' Ruth reassured them as she showed her warrant card. 'Don't want you to injure yourselves on our account. Where can we find Sonia Fletcher?'

'She's in the main office,' one of the men explained as he struggled under the weight of the carpet.

'Thanks,' Nick said as they made their way across the loading bay and inside the warehouse.

The interior was vast, stretching up about fifty or sixty feet into a vaulted ceiling. There were rolls of carpet stacked in piles. A forklift truck trundled past.

Over to their right there was a glass-fronted office with

three or four people inside, sitting at desks and working on computers.

Ruth spotted that Sonia Fletcher was at the desk closest to the door.

Fishing out her warrant card once more, Ruth opened the door and she and Nick went inside.

'Sonia Fletcher?' she said in a quiet voice.

'Yes?' she said as she pushed her reading glasses up onto the top of her head and frowned at them.

'DI Hunter, DS Evans, Llancastell CID. Okay if we have a word in private somewhere?'

Sonia rolled her eyes and groaned. 'Jesus. When I wanted your lot's help you were nowhere to be found were you? What's this about?'

Nick gave her a forced smile. 'It really would be better if we go somewhere a bit quieter,' he suggested as he looked around at the others in the office.

'If this is some tedious update about my husband's accident, then I'm not interested. Andy is dead. We're not going to get any justice for what happened to him so that's that.'

Ruth shot Nick a look. This was proving to be more problematic than she first imagined it would be.

Ruth took two steps towards Sonia, now aware that everyone in the office was listening to their conversation.

'Actually, we'd like to talk to you about an incident that happened the day before yesterday,' Ruth said. 'Or, if you'd like, we could all go to the station for a chat?'

Sonia shrugged, rolled her eyes and got up from her desk. She pointed to a nearby door. 'There's a staff room. We can go in there, but I'm very busy so you need to make it quick.'

Ruth exchanged a look with Nick. *Well, she's a little treat, isn't she?*

They followed Sonia as the other people in the office stared over in silence.

The staff room smelled of stewed tea and bacon sandwiches. Ruth and Nick sat on a small, two-seater sofa while Sonia plonked herself down on a hard, grey plastic chair.

Nick pulled out his notebook and pen.

Ruth looked over at Sonia. Her whole demeanour had changed. She looked nervous. It wasn't surprising. She clearly suspected that they were going to ask her about the incident at the Esso garage. However, Ruth wondered if she had been so enraged by her encounter with Martin Jones that she had followed him to the building site over in Heswall and killed him in a fit of revenge. It was obvious from some of the posts she'd put on social media that she hated him.

'Can you tell us where you were the day before yesterday at around 6.30am?' Nick asked as he sat forward in his seat.

Sonia frowned. Ruth wondered if she was going to come clean immediately or wait to see what they confronted her with.

'I don't know what you're talking about,' she said with a defensive shrug. 'I was in bed at that time of the morning.'

Don't lie to us. We haven't got time for that!

'Really?' Ruth said in disbelief. 'And you're sure about that are you?'

'Yes, thank you,' Sonia snapped. 'Why? Where the hell do you think I was?'

'We <u>know</u> you were at an Esso garage near Neston at 6.30am,' Ruth said calmly. 'We've got CCTV footage of you, Sonia. Do you want to tell us what happened?'

'I wondered if that dickhead would go and report it,' she sneered. 'Jesus! What a nasty little prick that man is.'

Nick frowned. 'I assume you're referring to Martin Jones.'

'Yes,' she growled. 'You know I am. I saw him in the garage and went over.'

'Why did you go over?' Ruth asked.

'Are you bloody joking?' She glared at Ruth angrily. 'Martin Jones is responsible for my husband's death. He forced him to go up in that crane even though he knew the weather was dangerous.'

Ruth sat forward and looked at her. 'We've seen the toxicology report on Andy. He had alcohol and Valium in his system. He wasn't in a fit state to be working that morning.'

'How dare you,' Sonia said as she scowled at Ruth.

'I'm just repeating what was in the report. And what the coroner concluded in his investigation.'

'Yeah, well they got it wrong. I saw Andy that morning and he was fine. There was nothing wrong with him.'

Ruth took a few seconds. It wasn't relevant at this stage as to Martin's guilt in Andy's death. They weren't there to investigate that.

'So, you went over and slapped Martin?'

'If he's going to press charges, I really don't care.' Sonia sighed. 'I'm glad I slapped him. It made me feel better.'

Ruth exchanged a look with Nick. She knew what he was thinking. Either Sonia Fletcher was an incredibly good actor, or she had no idea that Martin Jones was dead. Although the car fire had been reported in the press, the fact that Martin had been found in the back of his car and had been murdered hadn't been released to the press yet.

Ruth looked directly at Sonia, wondering what her reaction to her next statement would be.

'Did you see Martin once you'd left the petrol station?'

'No. Look, if you're going to arrest me, just get on with it.'

'Martin Jones is dead,' Ruth said calmly.

Sonia's eyes widened. 'What?' she said with a shocked, incredulous expression.

'We believe that he was murdered shortly after you saw him at that petrol station.'

'Bloody hell … Someone told me there was a car on fire at that site in Heswall the day before yesterday. Was that to do with what happened to Martin?'

'I'm afraid we can't discuss details of the case with you at this stage,' Ruth explained, 'but I do need you to account for your whereabouts between 6.30am and 8.30am on that morning.'

'That's easy.' Sonia gave a triumphant smirk. 'I was delivering a carpet to Birkenhead. You can check with the customer. That's why I was on The Wirral.'

'Don't worry,' Ruth said dryly. 'We will.'

Sonia shook her head. 'Martin Jones is dead, eh? Well, someone has done me and my family one hell of a favour.'

Ruth's instinct was that Sonia was telling them the truth and that she had no knowledge of Martin's death until five minutes ago.

Chapter 28

Ruth sat back in the chair in her office, took a long swig of hot coffee and took a few moments to herself. Her eyes moved across her desk to the photograph of her daughter Ella, now in her 20s. The photograph had been taken when Ella was only about eight or nine years old. She was wearing bright pink love heart sunglasses and a small band of daisies in her hair. Ruth had only just met Sarah, and they'd travelled down to a child-friendly festival called *Camp Bestival* that was held in the grounds of Lulworth Castle. It had been the first time that Ella had camped. To be honest, it was only the second or third time that Ruth had ever stayed in a tent. Ella was so excited because the *Pop Idol* winner, *Will Young*, was playing. She knew all the words to his No 1 single *Evergreen*. Ruth remembered that she and Sarah were more excited about seeing *Nile Rogers and Chic*. They had drunk too much cider and danced to *Good Times* with Ella sitting on her shoulders.

A figure appeared at her door. It was Kennedy.

'Boss, DI Gorski is here to see you,' she said, gesturing out to the CID office.

'Send her in,' Ruth said, sitting up straight.

It had been an hour since Ruth had called Gorski to update her on the CCTV from the petrol station of Sonia Fletcher, her assault of Martin Jones, and Ruth and Nick's subsequent conversation with her.

At that moment, Gorski appeared behind Kennedy.

'Thanks Jade,' Ruth said, and then gestured to Gorski. 'Come and sit down.'

'I've been over to see Steph Jones,' Gorski explained. 'I was driving through Llancastell so I thought I'd come and update you and see how the other half live across the border.'

Ruth smiled. 'Not much different over here. More sheep, more rugby and that's about it. Although if I'm honest, I've found the people in North Wales a lot more friendly than South London. But that's not a very high bar.'

Gorski laughed. 'My mum and dad are from the North East. Gateshead.'

'I thought I detected an accent.'

'You should be a detective,' Gorski joked dryly.

'I should.'

'Anyway, the people back home are way more friendly than where I work,' she explained.

Ruth took a moment and then looked at her. 'Actually, we have a development with Steph Jones that I probably should have updated you on earlier.'

'What is it?'

'One of my officers saw Steph and Lilly kissing last night. And I mean <u>kissing</u>.'

Gorski pulled a surprised face. 'Really? There's something going on between them?'

'To be honest, I had my suspicions before yesterday. Or

at least I was surprised by how close they seemed to each other.'

Gorski frowned as she processed what Ruth had just told her. 'Do we think this has anything to do with what happened to Martin?'

Ruth shook her head. 'I can't see it, can you? Steph and Lilly both seem to be genuinely devastated by his death. And I get the feeling that Lilly and he were very close, despite what's happened with Steph.'

Gorski nodded. 'The attack on Martin was brutal and horrific. Even if they were having some kind of affair behind his back, I can't see that would warrant killing him like that.'

'No, I agree,' Ruth said, and then shrugged. 'It's just a bit of a weird one.'

'Yeah, well it goes with the job, doesn't it?' Gorski said with a half smile. 'And I bet you've come across far weirder?'

'Oh yes. Definitely,' Ruth snorted.

Gorski sat forward in her chair. 'I went over to see Steph because I wanted to ask her about the accident involving Andy Fletcher again. She said that Martin hadn't talked about it much. And certainly not recently. It's just that my instinct is that the accident is key to what happened to Martin.'

Ruth nodded in agreement. 'Mine too.'

'But you and DS Evans were convinced that Sonia Fletcher was telling you the truth?'

'Unless she's an amazing actress,' Ruth replied.

'Has the name Huw Williams cropped up in your enquiries yet?' Gorski asked.

Ruth knew she'd seen the name but couldn't remember why.

'He was operating the cherry picker crane when the accident happened. Apparently, he and Andy had been best friends since they were at primary school together. Williams hasn't been the same since Andy died. And he blames Martin Jones for what happened. Might be worth a chat? He lives up in Gresford so I thought I'd let you guys handle that.'

'No problem,' Ruth said, glad that the working relationship with Gorski and the police on The Wirral was proving to be amicable and easy so far. 'Anything on your side that we need to know?'

'There have been a few significant thefts from the site in Heswall in recent months. Equipment and materials. Runs into thousands. That's why Headline Properties beefed up their security with extra gates and a fence.'

'Shame they didn't think to put in CCTV. Then we would have seen exactly what happened to Martin Jones,' Ruth pointed out.

'True. We've been digging around and there have been rumours that the thefts are an inside job from someone working at the site. The thieves seemed to know exactly how to get through the gates, when there was expensive equipment at the site, and where it was being kept.'

'I assume that Martin or someone at Headline Properties was aware of these rumours?'

'I don't know.' Gorski shrugged. 'We haven't checked that yet. But if Martin was on to whoever it was feeding this gang the information, or even if he'd confronted them, that could have put him in a lot of danger.'

Ruth nodded as she processed this. It was definitely a line of enquiry worth looking at.

Ruth narrowed her eyes. 'I'm guessing that you asked Steph about this?'

'Yes. She said that she wasn't aware of the thefts and that Martin had never mentioned them to her. But Lilly said that she remembered her brother telling her about it a few months ago. Martin said that he was going to stop whoever was stealing the stuff, even if it meant sleeping overnight at the site,' Gorski said, and then gave Ruth a meaningful look. 'Martin also said that if he found the people stealing his stuff, he was going to give them a good kicking.'

Nick came to the door, knocked and looked in. 'Boss, something I need to run past you.'

'Fire away.'

He gestured to the A4 printout he was holding. 'We've got a breakdown of Martin Jones' mobile phone records. He received six texts on the morning he was murdered. All from the same number. I've done a check and the number is registered to Ruby Allen, Martin's business partner.'

Ruth frowned. Ruby Allen had clearly told them that she'd had no contact with Martin for a few days.

Chapter 29

Ruth had called Headline Properties in Wrexham to check on Ruby Allen's whereabouts. She needed to ask her why she'd chosen not to tell them that she had exchanged half a dozen texts with Martin Jones on the morning of his murder. It seemed incredibly suspicious that she had hidden this from them when they explicitly asked her when she last had contact with him.

Having been informed that Ruby was working from home, Ruth and Nick made their way over to Rossett, a small village to the north of Wrexham close to the border with England.

Pulling up outside the detached house, it was clear that Ruby had done well for herself. There was a brand-new white Porsche Cayenne on the drive, and the house was large with extensive gardens.

Crunching up the gravel driveway to the front door, Ruth knocked on the door and took a step back.

Thwack!

Both their attentions were drawn to a noise from the side of the house.

'What was that?' Nick asked as he took a few steps back.

Ruth followed him. Maybe Ruby was out in the garden.

They saw a young man in his late teens chipping golf balls on the lawn to the side of the house. Ruth recognised him from the photo that she'd seen on Ruby's desk at the Headline Properties main office.

'It's her son,' she explained.

Looking at the front door, Ruth wondered why there had been no answer.

'Better knock again,' she sighed as she banged a little harder on the door.

Nothing.

She glanced at Nick and gestured. 'Come on.'

They made their way across the rest of the drive and approached the young man as he expertly chipped a golf ball which dropped with a little plop onto the grass.

Ruth and Nick pulled out their warrant cards. 'Hi there. Sorry to interrupt your game,' Ruth said in a friendly tone. 'We're police officers from Llancastell CID and we're looking for your mum. Ruby?'

'Oh right,' he said, looking a little scared by their presence. He had a floppy fringe and was wearing a baggy sports top and black Adidas joggers.

'Sorry, I didn't catch your name?'

'Oliver. Ollie.'

'Is your mum home?' Nick enquired.

'Oh yes. But if she's at the top of the house, sometimes she doesn't hear the front door.' Ollie was tall, lanky and still had the awkward gait of a teenage boy. 'I can let you in through the kitchen if you like?'

Ruth nodded and smiled. 'That would be great, thanks.'

'Your chipping looks pretty good,' Nick said as they followed Ollie round the back of the house. 'You play a lot?'

'Every chance I get.'

'What do you play off?'

'Eighteen. But I'm trying to get it down,' Ollie said, looking a little surprised to be having this conversation with a detective.

'Eighteen's pretty impressive. I just hack around a few times a year.'

Ruth shot Nick a surprised look. She had no idea that he had any knowledge of golf.

'It's just through here,' Ollie said politely as he opened the door to a huge kitchen.

'Thank you.'

Ruth and Nick went inside. The kitchen was bespoke, with rolled marble tops, coffee machine, large American style fridge etc …

This is nice, Ruth thought to herself with a slight feeling of envy.

'I'll just go and get her,' Ollie said awkwardly as he bounded out of the kitchen and down the hallway towards the staircase.

Ruth stared at Nick from under lowered brows.

'What?' he asked defensively.

'Since when were you an expert in golf?'

He grinned. 'You don't know everything about me. I like to have a few secrets that I can drop in every now and then. Keeps you on your toes.'

'Oh right,' Ruth said, giving a little laugh.

A few seconds later, Ollie returned with Ruby.

'Everything okay?' Ruby asked. 'Have you found the person who …' Then she stopped and looked at Ollie. 'Why don't you carry on with your golf, Ollie?'

'Yeah, no problem,' he said, and left through the door that they'd come in through.

'I don't want to talk about what's happened to Martin in front of Ollie,' Ruby said quietly. 'He really liked Martin, so he's quite upset about what's happened.'

'Of course,' Nick said empathetically.

'I'm afraid we don't have a suspect yet,' Ruth admitted, and then pointed to a large oak kitchen table and chairs. 'Okay if we sit down for minute. There's a couple of things we'd like to go through with you.'

'Erm, yes, of course,' Ruby said, and then glanced at her watch. 'I've got to go back for a zoom call at twelve?'

Ruth checked her watch. It was 11.20am. 'Don't worry. We'll be long gone before then.'

Ruby looked anxious as they all sat down.

'Oh sorry. Do you guys want a coffee or a tea?'

'We're fine, thanks,' Nick assured her.

Ruth had decided that she was going to use the tactic of 'provable lies'. Get someone to tell you something when you already know that you can prove they are lying. It usually put whoever it was immediately on the back foot.

'I just wanted to check the last time that you had any contact with Martin?' Ruth asked nonchalantly as if this was just a throwaway question.

Ruby narrowed her eyes. 'I'm sorry. I'm sure I told you that. I hadn't had any contact with Martin for a couple of days. We were both incredibly busy.'

Ruth looked directly at Ruby who looked uneasy. 'The thing is Ruby, we've looked at Martin's phone records. And you sent him six text messages the morning he was murdered.'

The colour drained from Ruby's face.

An awkward silence.

'Erm, yes. That's right. I'd completely forgotten about that.'

Ruth sat forward and gave her a quizzical look. 'Come on. You don't expect us to believe that do you? How could you forget that you'd sent six texts to him that morning?'

Silence again.

Ruby's face twisted and her eyes filled with tears.

'I'm sorry,' she whispered. 'I …'

Nick leaned forward and rested his forearms on the table. 'Whatever it was, it must have been very urgent for you to send six messages to him before 8.30am.'

Ruby gave a slight nod as her eyes roamed nervously around the room. Wiping her tears, she took a deep breath to try and calm herself.

'You're going to need to explain to us why you sent those messages, what was in them, and why you felt the need to lie to us,' Ruth said calmly.

'I know.' Ruby shook her head as she got upset again. 'But I don't think I can.'

Ruth gave her a hard look. 'Why? This is a murder investigation.'

'Whatever it is,' Nick said gently, '… you're going to need to tell us.'

Ruby nodded. 'I was texting him about the thefts that we'd had from the building site.'

'Right, yes,' Ruth said, but she was none the wiser. 'We're going to need to know a little more than that.'

'I'd heard a couple of rumours that someone who works for us had been tipping off a gang about the machinery, and when and where it was being kept on site.'

'And who was that?'

'His name is Huw Williams,' Ruby said reluctantly. 'He's worked for us for years. I didn't want to believe it.

And as it was only a rumour, I didn't want to tell you about the texts.'

'Huw Williams?' Ruth said. 'He was working the crane the day that Andy Fletcher was killed in the accident last year. Is that correct?'

'Yes, that's right.'

'We understand that Huw was a close friend of Andy's and that he was incredibly angry about what happened to him,' Nick said.

Ruby nodded.

'Didn't you think that there might be a connection between Huw's anger about the accident and him being involved in the robberies?'

'I've only known for a couple of days,' Ruby said. 'I didn't want to think that Huw would do that to us. I get on really well with him.'

Nick scratched at his beard on his jawline. 'What about Martin?'

'No. Huw held a real grudge against Martin over what happened to Andy.'

'Why did you think that Huw was involved in the robberies?'

'One of the contractors said he'd heard a rumour. He said that Huw has a drink problem, and that when he's drunk he shoots off his mouth. He'd said something in a pub a few weeks ago.'

Ruth looked over at Nick. It sounded like they needed to go and talk to Huw Williams.'

Chapter 30

Georgie was in the kitchen in the Jones' home in her role as FLO. Pouring boiling water into mugs, she made two teas. One for Steph and one for herself. Lilly hadn't arrived at the house yet, and Georgie was hoping to have a discreet conversation with Steph before she arrived. She needed to somehow broach what she had seen the night before.

Looking out of the kitchen window, Georgie could see that Steph was sitting out on the patio vaping. She was lost in thought.

As Georgie went to pick up the two mugs of tea, she spilled one on the work surface.

'Bollocks,' she muttered under her breath as she looked around for something to wipe it with.

There seemed to be no kitchen roll and no cloth by the sink.

Crouching down, she gave a groan. Bending down while pregnant was getting increasingly difficult.

Opening the door to the cupboard under the sink, she began to rummage around the clutter to find some kind of cloth.

Something tumbled out of the cupboard and hit the floor with a loud thud.

Georgie looked at it.

It was a Portmeirion souvenir tea towel. But there was definitely something wrapped up inside it. And it was very heavy.

Unfolding it carefully, she saw that inside the tea towel there was a steel claw hammer.

That's weird, she thought to herself. *Why is there a hammer wrapped up in a tea towel?*

She immediately became suspicious. Did it have anything to do with what had happened to Martin? She knew that he had been hit several times across the back of the head, but forensics had found that the wounds to his skull were about five inches long. From what she could see, neither side of the hammer would make such wounds.

She also got a distinct waft of something. Bleach. *Someone has bleached this hammer and then hidden it under the sink.*

Georgie took a couple of photos on her phone and then put the hammer back as she had found it until she could run it past Ruth. She didn't think that asking Steph about it was a very tactful thing to do at this stage of the investigation. And it didn't match the pathologist or forensic team's description of the murder weapon.

Finding a white dish cloth, Georgie wiped up the tea and headed outside with the mugs, still preoccupied by the discovery.

As she went out of the kitchen door, a lovely breeze blew against her face. She took a deep breath. Now that the first few months of her pregnancy were over, she was glad that her morning sickness had all but gone.

'Here we go,' she said, as she placed the mug of tea in front of Steph and sat down opposite her.

The garden was large and well-tended. There was a

football and a little goal with a net, and on the far side was a pink plastic slide. For a second, Georgie wondered about her own child and whether it would be a boy or a girl. She had no preference. As long as it was healthy, that's all that mattered to her.

Steph clearly spotted Georgie looking at the stuff in the garden. 'Do you know if you're having a boy or a girl?' she asked, as she gestured to Georgie's bump.

'No. I don't think I want to know.'

'What about your partner. What does he think?'

Her question stopped Georgie in her tracks. 'Actually, the father died quite recently. In fact, he didn't even know that I was pregnant.'

Steph shook her head. 'Oh God, I'm so sorry to hear that.'

'Thank you.'

Silence. Georgie's mind went back to the hammer that she'd found under the sink. It was definitely a weird one.

Steph took a long drag of her vape and then let out a huge cloud of vapour and gestured to it. 'Don't judge me.'

'After what you've been through, you do whatever you need to do,' Georgie reassured her.

Steph gave her a kind look. 'Sounds like we've both been through a difficult time.'

'Yeah. And it does get easier very slowly.' Georgie raised an eyebrow. 'No Lilly today?'

'She's doing some work this morning,' Steph explained. 'Then she's heading over here.'

'You two seem very close,' Georgie said, and watched for Steph's reaction.

'We are,' she replied, not giving anything away.

'I mean, you seem more like sisters.' Georgie wondered how she was going to manage to ask about what she'd seen the previous day.

'Yes. Lilly's the closest thing I have to a sibling. I'm an only child.'

Georgie made eye contact with her. There was no easy way of doing this. 'But it's never been more than that?'

Steph blinked for a few seconds as if she didn't quite understand what Georgie was getting at. Then the penny dropped and her face fell.

'What the hell are you talking about?' she snapped defensively.

'You are very close. And I'm asking if it's ever been more than a sister-in-law relationship?'

'Jesus!' Steph yelled. 'What the hell would make you say that?'

'I saw the two of you yesterday, when I was leaving. I saw you through the window to the living room.'

'So what?' Steph virtually spat out the words.

'You were kissing,' Georgie explained quietly. 'I saw you.'

Steph moved her chair back suddenly and then stood up. 'Don't be so bloody ridiculous. That's disgusting.'

Georgie watched as Steph stormed down the garden and into the house.

Then she turned back. 'And I want you out of this house.'

In Georgie's experience, it was only guilty people who reacted in such an extreme way.

Chapter 31

Ruth and Nick pulled into the Headline Properties building site in Heswall. The burned-out shell of Martin Jones' car had now been removed by the forensics team and there were various workmen in high-vis jackets moving windows into position on one of the houses.

Getting out of the car, Ruth and Nick looked over at a large man standing beside a small digger.

'We're looking for Huw Williams,' Ruth explained as she flashed her warrant card.

'Right you are.' Then he put his fingers to his mouth, gave an ear-splitting whistle, and gestured to a rotund man in a safety helmet who was sipping a mug of tea and smoking a cigarette. 'Huw? Over here,' he shouted in a thick Welsh accent.

'Thanks,' Ruth said, even though her ears were still ringing from his deafening whistle.

Huw came ambling over, already looking suspicious at their arrival.

'Yeah,' he said with a distrustful expression. 'You looking for me?'

'I wonder if you've got a couple of minutes to answer some routine questions?' Ruth said in a friendly tone.

'Do I have a choice?' he asked with a forced smile. His eyes were a little bloodshot and his face was puffy. He looked like he had a drink problem. Maybe that was why he and Andy Fletcher had been such good friends?

'Won't take long,' Nick reassured him.

As the digger started up, Ruth looked at him. 'Is there somewhere a bit quieter we can go?'

'Yeah. The office is over there,' he said over the noise of the digger.

They followed him across the uneven ground of the building site and up the steps of a Portakabin.

The office inside was cluttered. There were three desks with computers, and a man in a high-vis jacket was over by the photocopier.

'Can you give us a minute, Charlie?' Huw said to the man.

'Yeah, no problem.' Charlie walked past them and went outside.

Ruth pointed to two plastic chairs. 'Okay if we sit down?'

'Help yourself,' Huw replied in an unfriendly tone.

'Can you tell us where you were the day before yesterday between 6am and 9am?' Nick asked as he fished out his notebook and pen.

'I was at my caravan,' he replied curtly.

'And where is that?'

He perched himself against a desk and folded his arms defensively. 'White Sands caravan park in Porthmadog.'

'And there's someone who can vouch for that, is there?'

'Of course. I was with my wife,' he said with a shrug. 'Or ask any of the staff down there. They all know me.'

He then pointed outside. 'Jesus, you don't think I had anything to do with what happened to Martin?'

Ruth ignored his question. 'So, when did you get back?'

'Last night.'

'I'd like to ask you about an accident that happened here about a year ago. I understand that you were working on the crane when Andy Fletcher was killed, is that right?'

'Yes,' he said quietly, 'but he shouldn't have been up there.'

Nick stopped writing and looked at him. 'I understand that you and Andy were close?'

'He was my best mate,' he growled, 'and he'd still be here if it wasn't for …' Then he tailed off.

'If it wasn't for Martin Jones,' Ruth said, finishing his sentence for him.

'Yeah, exactly,' he snorted.

Ruth let his comment hang in the air for a moment.

Nick narrowed his eyes. 'I'm guessing you must have been pleased when you heard the news about Martin?'

'No,' he said defensively. 'No chance. You're not pinning that on me. I hated Martin for what he did to Andy. But there's no way I could do something like that to him.'

Ruth raised an eyebrow. 'Do you have any idea who might have wanted to harm Martin?'

'No.'

'And you're sure about that?'

'Yes,' he said anxiously.

'What do you know about the series of thefts that there have been from this site in recent months?'

'Nothing.' Huw shrugged, and his body language became even more closed off and awkward. 'The same as anyone else knows. It's a bloody pain in the arse and it's holding up the job.'

'You've heard the rumour that it's an inside job though?' Ruth said calmly.

'No, I haven't heard that.' Huw was getting increasingly twitchy.

'Come on, Huw. It's got to be an inside job. This gang knows when the expensive equipment is here, where it's being kept, and how to bypass some of the security measures,' Nick said sternly.

'What has this got to do with me?' Huw asked as he squirmed in his seat.

Ruth could see that he was now bright red and starting to sweat. His breathing was also fast and shallow. If she didn't know better, she'd think that he was about to have a panic attack. All the anger and hostility were now gone.

'Well, for starters, there is little love lost between you and Headline Properties. You blame them for the death of your best friend.'

'So what?' he said quietly.

'Your name has now come up on several occasions in relation to these thefts,' Ruth said, looking directly at him. 'Can you tell us why that is?'

'No. I don't know,' he said, sounding very edgy. 'I haven't got anything to do with it.'

Ruth stared at him and let the tension mount for a few seconds.

'Huw, we know that you're involved,' she said, and then just stared directly at him again.

He shook his head but his hands were shaky. He was struggling to get his breath.

Jesus, I hope he doesn't have a heart attack on us, Ruth thought, now feeling concerned.

Nick leaned forward. 'Come on, Huw. Whatever it is, you can tell us,' he said in a friendly tone.

Huw looked at the ground and shook his head adamantly. 'I can't tell you,' he whispered.

'What can't you tell us?' Ruth asked gently.

He blew out his cheeks and tried to suck in breath. 'I can't talk to you. I need to go.'

He turned and took a few steps towards the door.

'Huw, if you walk out of that door we'll be taking you to the station for questioning,' Ruth said.

He stopped in his tracks and turned back to them.

Ruth knew that whatever it was, Huw was incredibly scared of whoever was behind the robberies.

'Have you been threatened, Huw?' she asked.

He nodded but continued to stare at the floor, shaking.

'You need to tell us what's going on, Huw,' Nick said in a comforting tone. 'We can protect you.'

'No, no, you can't. They said that if I didn't help them, they'd hurt my family.' There were now tears in his eyes.

'You need to tell us everything you know,' Ruth said quietly. 'Then we can put these people behind bars. And if we need to, we can offer you protection.'

Huw trembled as he raised his head and looked at them both.

'I don't know what to do,' he said. He was completely broken.

'The men that are making you do this are never going to stop, you do know that?' Ruth explained. 'Now they've got their claws into you, they are going to keep using you until they don't need you anymore. And then you're expendable to them.'

Huw's eyes flitted nervously around as he understood what Ruth was implying.

'They're from Birkenhead,' he mumbled. 'They work out of the Hastings Scrap Yard up there.'

'We need names,' Ruth said as she shot a look over at

Nick. Her instinct was that Martin Jones' murder could be linked to this gang.

'I've dealt with a Callum,' Huw babbled, 'and a bloke called Gary.'

Ruth raised an eyebrow. 'Gary?'

'I don't know his surname.' Huw reached into his pocket. He pulled out a small black phone which he held out in his hand that was now shaking uncontrollably. 'They gave me this burner phone to use.' Then he looked at Ruth with pleading eyes. 'Please, I need you to protect my wife and daughters. They know where we live. I don't care what happens to me, but you need to get them to somewhere that's safe.'

Ruth nodded. 'Don't worry. If you continue to cooperate, we can put you and your family into protective custody tonight.'

'Yes, thanks.' Huw gasped. He was shaking.

'Was Martin Jones on to you?' Nick asked. 'Did he suspect that you were the person who was feeding this information to the gang?'

'I think so. I got the feeling that he suspected me. Just a couple of things that he said.'

Ruth gave him a dark look. 'And did you flag it up to someone in the gang that you thought Martin was on to you and what was going on?'

Huw closed his eyes and then nodded slowly.

'And what did they say to that?'

'Gary said that if Martin was sticking his nose into things, he would be dealt with.'

Chapter 32

An hour later, Ruth had called her contact in the Crown Prosecution Service to tell her what Huw Williams had told her. Even though it was a formality at this stage, Ruth needed to run putting the Williams family into protective custody past the CPS before talking to the Witness Protection Unit. The CPS gave her the go-ahead. She then called Gorski to tell her about Huw's confession and the links to the gang in Birkenhead. Ruth and Nick were due to meet with her at Arrowe Park nick in thirty minutes.

They parked up on Price Street to the north of Birkenhead. The area was run down, with some huge container warehouses for the docks that were only spitting distance from where they were sitting. Birkenhead was one of the poorest areas in the UK with a very high crime rate. People from Liverpool often referred to those across the water in Birkenhead as *Jedis*. It was said that it was because all the 'scallies' from Birkenhead were from the dark side and walked around with their hoods up.

As Ruth got out of the car, she stamped out her cigarette on the pavement and looked across at the Hastings Scrap Yard. When she had worked in the Met, anyone owning a scrap metal yard was synonymous with being 'a villain'. In fact, Eddie and Charlie Richardson, the most notorious gangsters from South London in the 1950s and 1960s, had worked out of their scrap metal yard in Camberwell. The Richardson gang ended up in a turf war with the Kray twins in the late 60s.

Nick gave Ruth a look, and they crossed the road to see if they could see anything. They weren't expecting to see any stolen equipment, but Ruth wanted to give the place the once-over before meeting with Gorski.

Looking around at the fence, Ruth saw that there was razor wire all the way around the top. There were also some very sophisticated CCTV cameras over the main office block and workshops.

'Pretty heavy security for a place like this?' Nick remarked.

'Yeah,' Ruth agreed sardonically. 'Maybe they're worried someone's going to run off with a tonne of scrap metal.'

Nick laughed. 'The last place I saw like this was a front for a lot of washing.'

Ruth knew what he meant. Yards like this were the perfect front for drug gangs wanting to launder their illegal money.

As they wandered across the yard, there was an eerie stillness. The only sound was the metallic crusher in the distance.

There didn't seem to be anyone around.

Suddenly, there was the thunderous sound of barking that made Ruth jump out of her skin.

About twenty yards away, two American XL bully dogs jumped up at the wire mesh of their enclosure, their mouths snapping and foaming.

'Afternoon officers,' said a chirpy voice in a Scouse accent.

Looking around, Ruth saw a tall man, 40s, shaved head, jewellery, tattoos and a Stone Island jacket. He was munching on what looked like a kebab.

'That obvious, is it?' Ruth asked dryly.

'It is to me, love,' he replied with a smirk before taking an enormous bite from the kebab.

'Bit early for a kebab,' Nick said.

'Nah, not these babies,' he said, shaking his head. 'You wanna get yourselves round to the Kebab House over there. Bloody lovely. Bit of chilli sauce and lemon.'

'Right,' Nick said, looking amused.

'We're looking for Gary Hastings,' Ruth said at a guess. The yard was called Hastings.

The man laughed ironically. 'Friend of yours, is he?'

Good guess, Ruth thought to herself.

'No, we just wanted a chat.'

'He's been away on holiday. Should be in later though. You wanna leave us your card or something?'

'No, it's okay,' Ruth said as she and Nick turned to go, 'and enjoy the rest of your kebab.'

'Don't worry, love, I will.' He gestured over the road. 'Get yourselves round there. Honest.'

Chapter 33

Kennedy and Price pulled into the White Sands caravan park. It was the end of the season and there was drizzle in the air. Kennedy knew that she was being a snob, but she found caravan parks in the rain a bit depressing.

'I've only just remembered,' Price said chirpily, 'but I came here as a kid. I was probably only about five or six.'

'Oh God,' Kennedy groaned sarcastically. 'And now you're going to tell me that was some time in the noughties, right?'

Price smiled and then pulled a face. 'Yep. I'm guessing about 2003.'

'Jesus,' Kennedy laughed. 'I'm not going to say anything about how young you are. I remember when I was new on the job. I was a probationer over in Chester and they put me with this sergeant who had been on the job for thirty years. He 'mansplained' everything we did as though I didn't have an ounce of common sense.'

'Thank you,' Price said gratefully.

Kennedy looked directly at him. He looked so bloody

young. 'But I must warn you, if you fuck up, I will hurt you.'

Price grinned. 'Consider me warned. Is this the time to tell you that I used to be North Wales under-16 judo champion?'

Kennedy frowned. 'Are you joking?'

'No, seriously. At one point they were talking about me going to the Olympics.'

'Right, well at least I know you can handle yourself,' she said, trying not to sound surprised. Price didn't look like a judo champion to her.

They got out of the car as the drizzle turned to full rain.

Grabbing her coat, Kennedy looked around for an office or someone to talk to. The rain started to run off her head and down her back.

'Bloody hell,' she growled.

'Over there,' Price said and pointed.

There was a middle-aged woman mopping the floor of the shower block.

Kennedy and Price jogged over.

Price groaned, and pointed down to his black loafers that were now covered in mud. 'My bloody shoes.'

'Yeah, don't be wearing stupid footwear like that again, Alfie,' Kennedy said, giving him a withering look.

Reaching the shower block, they took cover from the rain under the flat roof which jutted out.

The woman, who had stopped mopping as they approached, gave them a quizzical look.

They took out their warrant cards.

'DC Kennedy and DC Price, Llancastell CID,' Kennedy explained. 'We're looking for someone who might be in charge here.'

'Oh right,' the woman said, pulling a face. 'Erm,

Lennie is over in the shop. It's closed until later but if you bang on the shutters he'll open them.'

'Okay, thank you,' Kennedy said with a kind smile.

Turning around, they jogged back across the site and headed for the shop marked *White Sands Convenience Store*. There were metallic shutters that had been pulled down.

Kennedy banged loudly on the metal.

After a few seconds, she heard a man's voice. He had a thick North Wales accent.

'All right, where's the bloody fire?'

The shutters went up and a man in his 50s, grey beard, balding head, looked at them through his glasses.

Kennedy flashed her warrant card. 'DC Kennedy. And this is my colleague, DC Price. We're from Llancastell CID.'

'Llancastell, eh?'

'We did try to ring but it went straight to voicemail,' Price explained.

'Oh right, yeah. We're very short staffed at the moment. Couple off sick.'

'We're looking for Lennie?' Kennedy said.

'Aye, that's me,' he said with a jokey face. 'Bloody hell. What have I done?'

Kennedy gave Price a look as if to say, 'We've got a right one here.'

'Actually, we're trying to establish the movements of one of the owners here,' Price explained.

'Oh yeah,' Lennie said with a friendly expression. 'Who's that then? I've got to know most of the owners here over the years.'

'Huw Williams.'

Lennie furrowed his brow as he took in what she'd said.

'I'm confused,' Lennie said. 'Huw?'

'Do you know Huw Williams?' Price asked.

'Oh aye. Nice fella. Got a couple of daughters. He thinks the world of them,' he said with a nod. 'What do you need to know?'

'Huw has told us that he was here at his caravan until very early the day before yesterday.'

Lennie frowned and shook his head. 'Eh? Well, that's impossible.'

Kennedy narrowed her eyes. 'Why's that impossible?'

'Because Huw sold his caravan about six months ago. He said he had financial worries. In fact, I helped him sell it.'

'So, he wasn't here?' Price asked to clarify.

'No, Huw hasn't been here since he sold up.'

Kennedy and Price exchanged a look. Huw Williams had lied about his whereabouts at the time of Martin Jones' murder.

Chapter 34

Ruth and Nick were now sitting opposite Gorski in a meeting room on the ground floor of Arrowe Park nick. The room was basic and a little soulless, as most meeting rooms in police stations were. There were Venetian blinds at the window.

Sipping at her canteen coffee, Ruth looked over at Gorski who was thumbing through a file.

'I've had a call from one of my officers,' Ruth said. 'We checked Huw Williams' alibi for Monday morning. He claimed that he was at his caravan over in Porthmadog. The only problem being that he sold the caravan six months ago and hasn't been down there since.'

'Jesus,' Gorski said, shaking her head. 'He must have assumed that you weren't going to check.'

'That's the beauty of this job,' Nick said sardonically. 'We spend our lives listening to people lie to us.'

'Where is he now?' Gorski asked.

'He's in protective custody until we can confirm that he and his family can be registered with the Witness Protection Unit.'

'Yeah, well he won't be in protective custody for long if he's lying to us,' Gorski said dryly.

Ruth nodded. 'We'll go and speak to him and see what he has to say for himself.'

Gorski raised an eyebrow. 'You think he was involved?'

Ruth pulled a face. 'I don't think so.' She looked at Nick for a second opinion.

'I can't see Huw having it in him to murder Martin Jones, put his body in his car and set light to it. He was in pieces when we spoke to him earlier. I just think he's up to his neck in it and isn't thinking clearly.'

'Well, he'd better start thinking clearly or he's going to end up dead.' Gorski turned around a file. 'There's something that I need to show you.'

There was a photo of an enormous man in his early 50s with a bald head. He had gnarled features and the stature of a boxer.

'This is Gary Hastings,' Gorski explained. 'He's got a string of past convictions for violence, drug dealing, theft and extortion. I've spoken to the NCA and he's on their watchlist. They've been keeping an eye on Hastings Scrap Yard for the past eighteen months, but so far they haven't managed to find anything.'

The NCA stood for the National Crime Agency. They were the primary police unit dealing with organised crime.

Ruth pulled the photo towards her to have a look. 'It's not beyond the realms of possibility that Hastings and his gang were behind the robberies. And if Martin Jones got in their way, they got rid of him.'

Gorski nodded. 'Yes, in fact it's a very strong hypothesis about what happened to Martin. The only problem we've got is proving anything. Hastings and his associates are seasoned criminals so they will have done a good job of destroying any evidence.'

'Which is why they burned the car with Martin inside.'

'Exactly,' Gorski agreed, 'but we do have an informant who claims that Hastings is looking to fence the equipment stolen from the Headline site. Which means that it is being kept somewhere on the Hastings Scrap Yard site.'

'Are you thinking that we raid the yard to see what we can find?' Nick asked.

'Exactly,' Gorski said with an affirmative nod.

'I assume that we're taking no chances, and AFOs will be with us?' Ruth asked.

AFO stood for authorised firearms officers.

'I've already spoken to our Tactical Firearms Unit,' Gorski said as she looked down at her watch. 'I think we should move on this quickly so I'm suggesting we go in at 4pm?'

'That's fine by us,' Ruth said, looking at her watch.

Gorski looked at them both. 'I've made wearing bullet-proof vests mandatory for all my officers given Hastings' record and the intel from the NCA.'

Ruth and Nick shared a look. It had been a while since either of them had been on a raid that required firearms officers or bulletproof vests.

Chapter 35

Ruth, Nick and Gorski were now in the back of an armed response vehicle which was trundling up the road towards the Hastings Scrap Yard in Birkenhead. The inside of the ARV was stuffy and hot. They were sharing the vehicle with four authorised firearms officers in full combat equipment. Within the police, AFOs were referred to as 'shots', and they were clad in black helmets, Perspex goggles, balaclavas, Kevlar bulletproof vests, and Heckler & Koch G36C assault rifles. The G36C carried a 100-round C-Mag drum magazine and fired at the deadly rate of 750 rounds per minute. In an operation like this, the AFOs needed more firepower than the 9mm pistols or carbines that they usually carried. When there were operations involving OCGs on Merseyside, no one was willing to take any risks.

The armoured BMW X5 slowed to walking pace. Ruth peered outside and saw that there was an unmarked car of CID detectives from Arrowe Park nick parked up the street from the entrance to the yard. She also knew that there were four uniform patrol cars in nearby streets.

It had been a while since Ruth had been involved in an armed raid. She could feel her pulse starting to quicken as the adrenaline zipped around her bloodstream.

Her Kevlar bulletproof vest was heavy as it bounced against her shoulders. As always, it was way too big. She was a diminutive 5' 4", which meant even the smallest vest, with its heavy armour plating, jolted around her shoulders and left scratches and bruises.

Bloody hell, I'm getting too old to be doing stuff like this.

She thought of her initial plan to move to North Wales Police in 2017. In her head, she imagined a nice quiet desk-based job with low level crime. After all, how much crime could there be in Snowdonia and the surrounding area? Her colleagues in the Met had made jokes about sheep rustling, tractor theft etc … Of course, it hadn't turned out like that. There was as much crime in North Wales as anywhere else in the country. And now she was sitting in an ARV, wearing a bloody bulletproof vest, with a load of hairy-arsed AFOs on an armed raid. *The bloody irony*, she thought to herself.

Nick caught her eye. 'You gonna be alright to do this?'

'You do know that this is not my first rodeo?' she said caustically.

'Ha ha.' Nick rolled his eyes. 'I just meant with your ticker and everything.'

Ruth had had a cardiac arrest after being shot earlier in the year. However, there had been no lasting damage to her heart.

'The doctor gave me a clean bill of health,' she said with a raised eyebrow, 'so I've got a few years left in me before I need a Zimmer frame.'

'I didn't mean it like that,' Nick protested.

'I know,' Ruth laughed. 'I'm getting on, so I'm a bit sensitive about my age.'

For the next few minutes there was silence inside the ARV as it moved towards the entrance of the yard. Just the crackle of the Tetra police radio and the mumbled voice of Gold Command giving the driver instructions.

The ARV smelled of gun oil, male sweat, and stale cigarettes.

The driver spoke into the radio. 'Gold Command, Gold Command. Oscar Delta five, are you receiving, over?'

'Gold Command to Oscar Delta five. Receiving, go ahead. Over,' Gold Command acknowledged.

'Oscar Delta five. We have arrived at the target destination. Out,' replied the driver.

'Standby.'

The ARV stopped but Ruth knew that they were about to enter the yard. She shared a nervous look with Nick and Gorski.

The ARV moved forward slowly through the gates of Hastings Scrap Yard.

Ruth scanned the area over by the workshops, but the place seemed to be deserted.

The ARV came to a stop.

Ruth saw Gorski unclip her seatbelt and open the door.

Getting out slowly, she gazed over at the office and the workshops.

Nick frowned. 'No one at home,' he said sardonically.

Gorski clicked her radio on and spoke. 'Three-seven to Gold Command, we are approaching target location, over.'

In their well-rehearsed technique, the AFOs fanned out and moved swiftly towards the workshops, Portakabins and other buildings.

Except for the sound of the wind, the yard was eerily quiet and deserted.

A rusty oil can blew along the ground noisily in front of them.

Two huge white gulls flew from behind a pile of iron pipes and up into the air, eventually resting on the top, where they squawked and chattered noisily.

It's very quiet, Ruth thought. *Too quiet, maybe?*

There was a whoosh as the wind picked up again.

She felt uneasy.

Glancing to her right, she saw the AFOs fan out further as they moved into position, crouching low against the building. They weren't going any further until everything was secure.

Three of them reached to their belts and took out G60 stun grenades.

There was a movement of light from over by one of the Portakabins.

Ruth's heart now pounded against her chest.

Was someone watching them from over there? Did they already know they were here?

Her pulse quickened as she and Nick approached the doorway to one of the workshops.

She listened for a moment.

It really is too quiet, she thought.

She peered in, but the workshop was empty. There was an old shell of a car with no tyres up on bricks. There were tools and a workbench on the far side of the room.

Where the hell is everyone?

Taking a breath to calm her nerves, Ruth glanced back at the AFOs, who still hunkered down by the wall. One of them shook his head at Gorski to show he hadn't seen anything.

Gorski clicked her radio on as she took a few steps away from the workshop and glanced at Ruth.

'Gold Command, Gold Command from three-seven. Over.'

'Gold Command. Receiving. Over.'

'Three-seven. I'm at the target location, but we have no visual on suspects. Entry team is in final position, over.'

'Gold Command. Received. Proceed with caution—'

CRACK!

Before Ruth could react, pellets hit the ground beside her feet, throwing dust and dirt into the air.

Jesus!

The sound of a shotgun was deafening.

Nick grabbed hold of her bulletproof vest and pulled her to the ground.

'Bloody hell,' he gasped as they lay looking up.

A flash from a shotgun's muzzle over by the Portakabin.

'This is private property!' shouted a deep voice with a Scouse accent.

Ruth looked at Nick. 'We need to move. We're sitting ducks here.'

Nick gestured to the huge pile of iron pipes. 'There.'

Scrambling to their feet, they sprinted towards the cover of the pipes before skidding to the ground.

CRACK!

Shouting, glass breaking, a yell.

'Armed police, drop your weapons!' shouted an AFO.

Suddenly, there was some loud shouting.

'It's a bit late to start telling us you're busies, mate,' yelled a voice. 'How the fuck were we meant to know that?'

'Get your hands up and get down on your knees!' an AFO bellowed. 'Now!'

Something was going on, but Ruth couldn't see what from where they were hiding.

'Down on your knees now!' another AFO shouted.

Gorski looked over and gave them a reassuring nod. It was okay for them to come out from where they were taking cover.

Ruth and Nick dusted themselves down and came tentatively from behind the pile of iron pipes.

Two figures were now kneeling on the ground in front of the Portakabins with their hands up.

One of them was Gary Hastings.

The AFOs had their guns trained on them both as they moved in, pushed them face down onto the floor, and cuffed their hands behind their backs.

There were two shotguns lying on the ground beside them.

Hastings was grinning. 'My brief is gonna have a field day over this.'

'Shut up!' shouted one of the AFOs.

Ruth gave Nick a look and blew out her cheeks. That had been a little more scary than she'd anticipated.

Chapter 36

Two hours later, Gorski pressed the button on the recording equipment and said, 'Interview conducted with Gary Hastings, 6pm, Interview Room 2, Arrowe Park Police Station. Present are Gary Hastings, Detective Inspector Ruth Hunter, Gary Hasting's solicitor Darren Brady, and myself, Detective Inspector Karolina Gorski.'

Hastings sat with his legs wide apart with the kind of amused smirk that Ruth had seen so many times before on hardened criminals. She wasn't sure, but she suspected that he would be going 'no comment' for the interview. That's what men like Hastings usually did.

'Gary,' Gorski said. 'I'm just going to check a couple of details with you. You are Gary Anthony Hastings. Date of birth, 30th August 1971. Given address is 23 St Mary's Avenue, Birkenhead. Is that correct?'

Hastings stared at the wall behind them and sighed loudly. 'No comment.'

'And you understand that you have been arrested on suspicion of the murder of Martin Jones, attempted murder of a police officer, and burglary?'

Hasting's solicitor leaned in and whispered something to Hastings.

'Yes,' Hastings said reluctantly.

Ruth reached for a folder in front of her. She took out a photograph that officers had taken earlier at the Hastings Scrap Yard. 'For the purposes of the recording, I'm showing the suspect Item Reference 898G. This is a photograph of various pieces of building machinery and equipment.' She turned the photograph so Hastings could look at it. 'Is there anything you'd like to tell us about this equipment, Gary?'

Hastings took a second to answer and then said, 'No comment.'

'Would it surprise you to know that all of this equipment has been stolen from the Headline Properties housing development site at Heswall in the past four months?' Hastings was still staring at the wall.

'No comment.'

Gorski leaned forward. 'I think it's safe to say that as this machinery and equipment was found on your premises, you stole it, Gary. Is that a fair assumption?'

Hastings ran his hand over his bald scalp. 'Do you know how many contractors have access to that site every day? Anyone could have come in and hidden that stuff there. Nothing to do with me.'

'But you stole it, Gary,' Gorski said.

'No, I didn't. And anyway, you can't prove it,' he said arrogantly. 'And the CPS is never going to take this to trial with no evidence. You've got no chance, love.'

Ruth was worried that what Hastings had said was true. The only thing that linked him directly to the stolen machinery was Huw Williams' statement. She pulled out another photograph and turned it to show Hastings. 'Can you tell me if you recognise this man please, Gary?'

Hastings couldn't help but move his eyes over to the photo. Then he shrugged. 'No comment.'

'This man's name is Huw Williams. He works for Headline Properties as a deputy site manager. It is his testimony that you threatened his safety and the safety of his family if he didn't feed you information about the security at the Heswall site, along with details of building machinery and equipment, and where it was being stored. Is there anything you'd like to say about that?'

Hastings gave a snort. 'No comment.'

'Are you saying that Huw Williams is a liar and that he didn't pass you any details about the site in Heswall?'

'No comment.'

Ruth pulled out another photograph. 'Could you look at this photograph for me please?'

Hastings took a few seconds and then moved his eyes down to look at it.

'This man is Martin Jones. He was a co-owner of Headline Properties. And he was murdered at the Heswall site on Monday morning. Is there anything you'd like to tell us about that?'

Hastings frowned and then rubbed his nose as if the photo and the question had rattled him a bit.

'No comment,' he said, but something was definitely up.

Gorski narrowed her eyes and looked over at Hastings. 'It is our belief that Martin Jones had discovered what Huw Williams was doing. That he was tipping you and your gang off. And Martin Jones was going to expose Huw Williams and you to the police as being behind the burglaries. Is there anything you'd like to tell us about that?'

Hastings frowned. 'Nah,' he said in a thick Scouse accent. 'You are well off on that, love.'

Ruth raised an eyebrow. 'Huw Williams told us that

when he flagged up that Martin Jones was suspicious about his involvement in the robberies, you told him that Martin would be 'dealt with'. Is that true?'

'No comment.'

Hasting's solicitor leaned in again, and he and Hastings spoke in hushed voices for nearly a minute.

'Gary, we know that you killed Martin Jones on Monday morning to stop him from going to the police,' Gorski said. 'And we're going to prove it. So, why don't you save everyone a bit of time and tell us what happened?'

Hastings sat forward and laughed. His gaze moved from Gorski to Ruth. 'Fucking hell, what are you two clowns doing running this investigation, eh? If I murdered this Martin Jones on Monday morning,' he said, pointing to the photograph, 'how do you explain me being on a flight from Ibiza that didn't get in until midday on Monday? It was me 50th birthday celebration, so I was with me mates and me family. Just ask them. We had a great time. And I had nothing to do with no murder, so you need to go and look somewhere else, all right?'

Ruth gave Gorski a frustrated look. If Hastings' alibi checked out, then they were back to square one. Unless Huw Williams was the killer, and that didn't seem likely.

Chapter 37

It was the following morning as Ruth marched across the CID office towards the scene board. 'Right everyone. Thank you for coming in this early. As you're all aware, this is a very fast-moving case so let's get up to speed please.' She went to the board and pointed to a photo. 'Martin Jones. Let's go through this methodically. Who has a motive for killing him?'

Nick pointed to another photo. 'Sonia Fletcher has motive. She blames Martin for pressurising her husband, Andy Fletcher, to go up in a crane during bad weather, and the subsequent accident in which he was killed.'

'Okay,' Ruth said. 'And we know that she has waged a campaign ever since to get Martin prosecuted for negligence as well as trolling him on various social media platforms.'

Price looked over. 'And we have the CCTV where she confronts and then slaps Martin the morning that he was murdered.'

'True,' Ruth agreed, 'but I've got Sonia down as a

pretty smart woman. If the encounter with Martin sent her into a rage, surely she would realise that the CCTV footage at the garage would have picked up the altercation with him?'

Georgie shrugged. 'Not if she really did lose her head and wasn't thinking straight. We don't know what Martin said to her at the petrol station. Did he provoke her? Did he say something about her husband? Maybe that's what wound Sonia up, and she decided to follow him and murder him.'

Nick didn't look convinced. 'I'm not sure about that. My instinct was that Sonia was genuinely surprised when we told her that Martin had been killed. And I admit that I've been wrong about that sort of thing before, but not often.'

'I agree,' Ruth said. 'My instinct was the same as yours, so we'll put Sonia Fletcher on the back burner.' She pointed to another photo. 'What about Steph and Lilly Jones?'

Georgie lifted her pen to signal that she had something to say. 'Steph and Lilly are having some kind of relationship.'

Ruth raised an eyebrow. 'And Steph didn't react very well when you asked her about it?'

'No, she flipped. She got very angry and stormed off. And since then, she's demanded that I be removed as the FLO.'

Kennedy chipped in. 'Do you think that her reaction was over the top?'

'Yeah, completely,' Georgie said. 'I know what I saw.'

'She doth protest too much,' Nick said.

A few blank faces.

'It's *Hamlet* I think,' he said with a shrug.

'And what about this hammer under the sink?' Ruth asked.

'It's a claw hammer.' Georgie pointed to one of the post-mortem photos up on the board. 'It doesn't fit the pattern of the wounds on Martin's skull. But it was definitely hidden in a tea towel and had been bleached. It just seemed weird.'

Ruth frowned as she took all this in. 'Do we really think that if Steph and Lilly are having some kind of relationship, they would plot to murder Martin?'

'Having spent time with them both, I can't see it,' Georgie admitted. 'They've both seemed utterly devastated by his death. I haven't seen anything that hints at guilt or that they're hiding anything to do with his murder.'

'Okay, we'll leave that,' Ruth said and then looked at the board again. 'Which leaves us with Huw Williams and Gary Hastings. My instinct is that this is where we need to look. Martin was killed because he discovered that it was Huw who was tipping off Gary Hastings and his gang about the machinery and the equipment on the site and how to bypass the security system. But we've checked with Liverpool John Lennon Airport and Gary Hastings did travel on a flight from Ibiza with friends and family which landed at midday.'

A phone rang on a desk and Kennedy went to answer it.

'So, Hastings didn't murder Martin,' Price said, thinking out loud.

'No,' Ruth replied, 'but he could have hired someone to do it. In fact, if you want to make sure you have a rock-solid alibi for a murder, make sure you're on a flight while the hit takes place.'

Nick gave a sarcastic look. 'Yeah, I don't think it was coincidence. Do you?'

Kennedy looked over. 'Boss, it's the front desk. Apparently, Huw Williams has left his protective custody and needs to talk to you urgently. He's downstairs.'

Ruth gave Nick a quizzical look. 'Right … we'd better go down there and see what he has to say.'

Chapter 38

Twenty minutes later, Ruth pressed the button on the recording equipment and said, 'Interview conducted with Huw Williams, 9.30am, Interview Room 1, Llancastell Police Station. Present are Huw Williams, Detective Sergeant Nick Evans, Duty Solicitor Bradley Kirk, and myself, Detective Inspector Ruth Hunter.'

Ruth wasn't sure why Huw had left his protective custody or why he was now at Llancastell nick to talk to her, but she wanted to make the interview official.

Huw fiddled nervously with his hands as he sat hunched over the table.

'Huw,' Ruth said calmly. 'We are recording this interview today and you are currently under caution. That means that anything you do say here can be used in the future as evidence in a court of law. Do you understand that?'

Huw nodded, but the blood had drained from his face and he looked grey. 'Yes,' he whispered.

If Ruth was going to make an educated guess, then

Huw or a member of his family had been got at by Hastings or one of his associates.

'Now you've chosen to turn down our offer of protective custody for you and your family,' Ruth said gently, 'can you tell us why?'

'I'm going to withdraw what I told you yesterday,' he said, his voice trembling with anxiety.

Nick narrowed his eyes. 'You want to withdraw your statement?'

Huw was so nervous he could hardly look at them. 'Yes. Everything I've told you was a lie.'

'You mean you made the whole thing up?'

'Yes … Yes, that's right. I did,' he stammered.

Ruth sighed. 'Don't be ridiculous, Huw. How could you possibly make up something like that? What are you talking about?'

'I don't care. I'm retracting everything I told you.' Huw then looked at the duty solicitor. 'I can do that, can't I?'

The duty solicitor nodded.

'Why are you doing this, Huw?' Ruth asked in a kind tone. 'I can see that you're scared, but this is going to make things worse.'

'No, it won't,' he mumbled. ' I just don't want to talk about it.'

Ruth took a few seconds to process this. 'My assumption is that somehow Gary Hastings or one of his associates has managed to speak to you in the last twenty-four hours. Is that correct?'

'No.' Huw shook his head, but she could see that he was lying. 'No, this is my decision. I don't want to say anything else.'

Nick sat forward. 'My guess is also that whoever did contact you, told you that you and your family wouldn't be safe in police protective custody. Or in any Witness Protection Scheme. Is that right?'

Huw didn't answer but instead he just looked at the floor.

'Is that what you were told, Huw? That they would find you and your family wherever you went? And the only way for you to be safe is to come here and retract everything you've told us and say that it was a lie and that you made it up. Is that what happened?'

'No,' he whispered without looking up.

Ruth looked at Nick. Even though Huw's evidence didn't get them any closer to finding out who actually murdered Martin Jones, it did mean that Gary Hastings would be charged with intimidation and burglary. Given Hastings' criminal record, he would be given a relatively long prison sentence.

Huw leaned into the duty solicitor and they talked in hushed voices.

'My client has said everything that he wants to say today,' the solicitor explained, 'and if there is nothing more, then I'd like him to be given permission to leave.'

Ruth gave Nick a frustrated look. Huw seemed adamant about his intention to retract everything he'd told them, and they could see that there was no way that he was going to give evidence against Gary Hastings.

Chapter 39

Ruth and Nick had been asked to go over to Arrowe Park nick for a meeting with Gorski and officers from the NCA. Ruth had been mulling over Huw Williams' decision to withdraw his statement, refusal to give any evidence against Gary Hastings or his associates, and therefore to withdraw himself and his family from police protective custody. Even if he had been threatened, it seemed naïve to think that he wasn't now in grave danger.

Nick parked in the car park. Ruth gestured to the cigarette she was smoking. 'Mind if I finish this before we go in?'

Nick shrugged as he buzzed down the driver's window. 'Knock yourself out.'

Taking a deep drag, Ruth blew the smoke out of the passenger window that was already open.

'There's nothing we can do to protect Huw Williams, is there?' she said rhetorically.

'No, there isn't,' Nick agreed, 'but I think his life is in danger and he needs to stay vigilant.'

'You know I was asked to join the National Crime

Agency back at the end of 2013 when it was established at Scotland Yard?' Ruth said, thinking back.

'No, I didn't know that.'

'I'd been heading up a task force to deal with the growing gang violence in South London. We'd had Operation Trident since the late 90s to tackle 'black on black' gun crime, and that was focused on Lambeth where I was based. And Brent. But it didn't seem to make any difference, and it was clear that the drug gangs were getting more organised and more violent.'

'But you didn't join the NCA?' Nick asked.

'No. I was all set to. I'd wanted to do something different and have a fresh challenge. I even had an interview lined up.'

'What happened?'

'Sarah went missing.'

'Of course.'

'5th November 2013.' Even though Sarah was back and safe, the thought of the day that she'd vanished off the face of the earth still made Ruth shudder. 'The ironic thing was that my interview was due for 6th November. And on the evening of the 4th, Sarah had done a mock NCA interview with me at our flat. You know, running through possible questions. Of course, when she went missing I couldn't concentrate on anything else and the whole thing just passed me by.'

'Sounds like you might regret missing the opportunity.'

'I do,' Ruth said without hesitation. 'There was nothing I could have done. Sarah had vanished. And I never really got over that until we found her.' She turned her head to Nick. 'Jesus, do you remember when we went to Paris to get her. Well, you came out to help me.'

Nick raised an eyebrow ironically. 'Yeah, I could hardly

forget that. I don't know how any of us got out of there alive.'

Ruth smiled. 'We've been through a lot, me and you, haven't we?'

'What's brought all this on?' Nick gave her a quizzical look. 'Are you ill or something?'

Ruth laughed. 'No.'

'You've rethought retiring?'

'No. Nothing,' she said with a reassuring grin. 'I'm just getting soft, and when you get to my ripe old age you sometimes take stock of your life.'

Nick looked out at the stark, concrete police station and car park.

'Even in the car park of Arrowe Park nick on The Wirral?' he joked.

'Yes,' Ruth chortled. 'Even here.' Then she tapped his shoulder. 'Come on, nobhead, let's get out and see what the NCA has to say.'

'Nobhead?' Nick asked with a look of mock offence.

'I'm sure you've been called worse,' Ruth said as she got out of the car and slammed the door shut.

Nick gave her a knowing look. 'You know if I was Gen Z, I would accuse you of a 'microaggression', report you to HR, and then have a day off for my poor mental health.'

Ruth shook her head. 'Well thank God you're not Gen Z, eh?'

Chapter 40

Price and Kennedy were in the canteen getting coffees. Kennedy was growing to like Price. She had been miffed when Ruth had first asked her to 'babysit' him, but it was becoming clear that he didn't really need babysitting. He had more common sense than most 'newbies' that Kennedy had encountered. Plus, she needed to remember how 'green' she had been when she was a probationer, or in her first few months when she had worked over in Chester CID. In fact, if she was honest, she was probably a few steps behind where Price was at this moment.

'I'll get this,' she said, pointing to his black Americano.

'Sure?'

'Of course.' Kennedy used her prepaid card on the machine by the till.

'Thanks,' Price said. 'Coffee is a lot better here than in Prestatyn.'

'Hey, I used to work at Chester,' she said with an amused smile, 'and you know how posh they are over there? Skinny, decaff mocha with roasted Ethiopian free trade beans.'

He laughed. 'That's the English for you. Entitled wankers.'

'Erm, I'm English,' she said jokingly. 'So, watch it newbie.

'Ooops,' Price said, pulling a face.

'Don't worry, I'm not particularly proud to be English. A kid cut me with scissors at school to see if my blood was red because I was black.'

'Jesus!' Price said as they went out through the double doors of the canteen.

'And when I first arrived at Chester Town Hall nick,' she continued, 'my sergeant asked where I was from. So, I said 'England'. Then he asked, 'but where are you really from?' So, I told him. 'Streatham.''

Price laughed.

'But he wasn't having it. Eventually I asked him, 'Are you asking what my heritage is?' He said, 'Yes, heritage, that's it.' So I said, 'I assume you ask every new copper what their heritage is. You know, are you a bit Irish or Scottish? Do you have any Scandinavian in your DNA? That kind of thing.''

Price grinned. 'What did he say to that?'

'He gave me a sarcastic laugh and walked off,' Kennedy replied as they got to the top staircase at the back of the nick and then headed along the first-floor corridor towards the CID office.

'My Dad's a bit of a bugger when it comes to the whole anti-English thing,' Price admitted as they went in through the double doors of CID and headed for their desks. 'He used to pretend he only spoke Welsh when English tourists asked him for directions.'

Kennedy laughed as she plonked herself down at her desk and logged on to her computer. She immediately saw that Martin Jones' bank statements had been sent over in full detail.

Scanning down the dates, she saw a series of payments at a pub called the Pant-yr-Ochain in Gresford on the Sunday evening before Martin Jones was murdered. From the amounts spent, it was clear that he hadn't been alone. There might be a totally logical explanation, but it also might be worth checking out.

'Alfie?' she said, getting up from her desk.

'Yes?'

'Come on, we're going to the pub.'

'Nice one,' he answered with a smile as he got up from his desk.

She laughed. 'Yeah, don't get too excited, we're chasing a potential lead.'

Chapter 41

Ruth and Nick walked into the meeting room on the ground floor of Arrowe Park nick that they'd been to previously. Gorski was already sitting at the table with two other detectives who Ruth assumed were from the NCA.

'Hi guys,' Gorski said, getting up. 'This is Detective Sergeant Stuart Caulfield and Detective Inspector Sue Storey from the NCA.'

'Hi there,' Ruth said as they all shook hands and sat down. 'Detective Inspector Ruth Hunter and Detective Sergeant Nick Evans, Llancastell CID.'

'Right, if we can get straight down to it,' Gorski said.

'We have bad news,' Ruth said, pulling a face. 'Huw Williams arrived at our station this morning. He wants to retract his statement from yesterday. He's not willing to give any evidence against Gary Hastings or his associates. And he's taken his family out of police protective custody.'

'Bloody hell,' Caulfield said in frustration.

Storey looked at them. 'Someone got to him?'

Nick nodded. 'That's what we suspect. He wouldn't tell

us. And he maintains now that everything he told us yesterday was a lie and that he made the whole thing up.'

'Shit,' Storey sighed.

'We've had Hastings under surveillance for over a year on and off,' Caulfield explained.

'Drugs?' Ruth asked.

'That's what we think, but we're struggling to find anything to pin on him. Although we've got him for discharging a firearm at police officers, his brief maintains that officers didn't make themselves known.'

Nick shook his head. 'What?'

'Plus, he's got licences for those shotguns. His brief is claiming that Hastings was acting in self-defence.'

'Are you joking?' Nick growled.

'I wish I was. We can't prove that Hastings stole the machinery and equipment found at the yard either. At worst, he's going to get a suspended sentence for reckless use of a firearm. But I don't know if he'll even get that.'

'Which is ridiculous,' Ruth stated. 'It's a miracle that no one was killed.'

'That's why we were counting on Huw Williams' testimony against Hastings so we could convict him of intimidation,' Storey said, sounding frustrated. 'Plus, we'd have a much better chance of pinning the theft of the machinery on him.'

'Do we have anything else that might link him to Martin Jones' murder?' Ruth asked.

Caulfield nodded and reached for the laptop beside him. 'Funny you should ask that. One of our surveillance teams got this a week before Martin's murder. It was two days before Hastings flew to Ibiza. They assumed it was a drug deal, but it was only cash that Hastings handed over.'

Caulfield pressed a button, and footage from a hand-held police video camera started to play.

The video showed a huge car park with a series of empty bays.

'This is Broughton Retail Park,' he explained.

A white van drew up and parked. A few seconds later, a black Range Rover Sport parked one space away.

The door to the Range Rover opened and Gary Hastings got out. At the same time, the door to the van opened and a short, stocky middle-aged man got out.

Hastings and the man shook hands and chatted. Then Hastings reached into his pocket, pulled out an envelope and handed it to the man.

They both got back into their vehicles and drove away.

Ruth peered at the screen. 'There's writing on that van. Do we know what it says?'

'Baker & Sons Decorating,' Storey said. 'Based over the border in Buckley.'

Nick pointed to the stocky man. 'And do we know who that is?'

'We're assuming that it's Kevin Baker. He's the registered owner of the van and the decorating company.'

Ruth frowned. 'And why are we so interested in Kevin Baker if he's a decorator?'

'Kevin Baker is ex-military. SAS, Gulf War.'

'Does he have a record?' Nick asked.

'No,' Storey admitted. 'But he did work as a mercenary for a few years in South America until he got shot and injured.'

'And we're wondering if Hastings hired Baker to kill Martin Jones while he and his cronies were over in Ibiza,' Caulfield said. 'It's a bit of a long shot, but it's all we've got to go on at the moment I'm afraid.'

Ruth looked at Nick. 'We'd better go and have a chat with him.'

Chapter 42

Kennedy and Price pulled into the car park of the Pant-yr-Ochain which was a lovely country pub on the outskirts of Wrexham. They made their way across the car park and went in. It was fashionably decorated inside and there were large doors leading out to an enormous terrace garden and lake.

Pulling out her warrant card, Kennedy went over to a young woman behind the bar.

'Hi there,' Kennedy said in a quiet voice. 'We're police officers from Llancastell CID. I wonder if the manager is around?'

The young woman nodded. 'Yes, that's James. I'll just go and get him for you.'

'Thank you,' Kennedy said with a kind smile.

'Nice place,' Price said, gesturing to the inside of the pub. Then he looked at the blackboard on the wall. 'Today's special. Pan-seared pork ribeye with chimichurri butter, fondant potato, roast onion, cherry tomatoes. Not something you'd find in my local Weatherspoon's,' he joked.

Before Kennedy could reply, a handsome man in his 30s approached.

'Hi there,' he said in a very middle-class accent. 'I'm James. I'm the manager here. How can I help?'

'We're trying to establish if one of your customers who was here on Sunday 22th August was alone,' Kennedy explained. 'Do you have CCTV?'

James gestured up to the corner of the ceiling and a small, black CCTV camera. 'Yes, we do. Would you like to come to my office and we can take a look?'

Kennedy nodded. 'Yes, that would be very useful.'

They followed James through the bar, down a small corridor and into an office.

He gestured to two chairs opposite a desk and computer. 'Would you like to sit down?'

'Thanks,' Price said.

'Okay, let's have a look, shall we?' James sat at his desk and started to use the mouse and tap buttons on his computer. 'Here we go. What time do you think this person might have been here?'

'The first drinks or food were bought on a card at 6.33pm,' Kennedy replied.

'Okay.' James pushed the large computer monitor around so that Kennedy and Price could see the CCTV footage. 'This is 6.30pm.'

Price leaned forward and peered at the screen. 'There,' he said and pointed.

Kennedy could see Martin Jones standing at the bar. He took two drinks from the bar and walked over to a seat by a window. There was someone sitting opposite him at the table. They were wearing a navy New York Yankees baseball cap, but because of the high angle of the CCTV camera, it was impossible to see their face.

Kennedy looked at James. 'Could you pause it there please?'

'No problem.'

Kennedy stared at the screen. 'That's not Steph Jones, is it?'

The person's height and stature looked wrong for it to be Martin's wife.

'No, I don't think so,' Price said. 'I can't even see if it's a man or a woman to be honest.'

Kennedy squinted. 'I think it's a woman.'

James looked at the screen. 'Hard to tell,' he admitted.

'Can we play this forward to see what happens? Maybe at a higher speed?' Kennedy suggested.

James started to play the footage forward at four times the normal speed.

Martin and whoever was sitting opposite him were deep in conversation. The other person reached out and took his hand and they held hands for a while.

'Can you stop it there please?' Kennedy asked as she looked again.

'There's definitely something going on,' Price stated.

Kennedy looked at James. 'Is there any way of making the image bigger?'

He shook his head. 'Sorry, it's pretty basic.'

'No problem,' she said. 'Can we carry on?'

The footage continued. Martin went to get more drinks from the bar.

After a few more minutes, it was clear that he was arguing with the person opposite. It looked like he was shouting, as several customers looked around.

'I don't suppose you remember anyone rowing in the pub on that Sunday?' Price asked.

'Sorry,' James replied with a shrug. 'It's not that unusual I'm afraid.'

Then the footage showed Martin getting up from his seat and marching out of the pub. The person he'd been with followed him out.

James paused the CCTV.

'I guess that's it?' Kennedy said, frustrated that they hadn't been able to spot who Martin had been arguing with.

'Actually, we have CCTV in the car park,' James said. 'Do you want to have a look? They would have come out into the car park when they left.'

'Great,' Kennedy said, feeling less discouraged.

A few seconds later, James tapped a few buttons and the CCTV footage of the car park appeared. It was still light outside.

They watched as Martin came out of the pub clearly still arguing with whoever he'd met.

However, the person's face still wasn't visible because of the baseball cap.

'Bollocks,' Price muttered under his breath. Then he looked at James. 'Sorry.'

James laughed. 'I've heard worse.'

The CCTV camera had a small splash of mud or dirt on it which obscured the bottom left of the screen. However, they could clearly see Martin getting into his car and slamming the door angrily.

Kennedy's eye was drawn to a car opposite – a red Mini Clubman with a personalised plate – for no other reason than it was exactly the same car as she had.

Then they watched as the person Martin had been arguing with jumped into a white Audi A3, but most of it was concealed by the dirt on the camera.

Kennedy looked over at Price who was scribbling in his notebook. 'Can you see that plate?'

'Sort of,' Price said, tapping his notepad with his pen. 'I've got the first part but that's all.'

'We'll have to run a partial plate through the DVLA and see what they can give us,' Kennedy said. 'But it's a white Audi A3, so that definitely narrows it down.'

Chapter 43

Ruth and Nick turned into a side road close to the centre of Buckley, which was a town in Flintshire, North Wales. It was about two miles north east of Mold, and eleven miles directly north of Wrexham. It was the second largest town in the area and its name dated back to the 12th century. The word *Bokkeley* meant 'a clearing of bucks' in Old English, and given its proximity to the English border that's what most people believed it was derived from.

As they drove down the small residential road, Ruth noticed a white van coming along the other way. She recognised it from the NCA video and saw the bright blue lettering on the side – *Baker & Sons Decorating*.

'That's him,' Ruth said, pointing. 'He must have just left home.'

'Right, I'll swing round and we can pull him over.' Nick applied the brakes and turned the steering wheel vigorously.

Within a few seconds they were behind the van as it turned left onto Liverpool Road, seemingly oblivious to their presence behind.

Ruth looked over at Nick. 'Actually, maybe we should follow him and see where he goes and if he meets anyone.'

'Sounds sensible.' Nick turned left and continued to follow the van.

The van then turned right and then hard left, and then left once again which basically brought them back up to Liverpool Road.

Ruth and Nick exchanged a confused look.

Nick frowned. 'What the hell was that all about?'

'Maybe he knows we're following him,' Ruth suggested.

'Yeah, well if he's just a decorator from Buckley, there would be no reason to think you were being followed by us, would there?' Nick pointed out.

'It's definitely suspicious,' Ruth agreed.

Suddenly, the van's tyres screeched as it lurched forward and began to increase speed rapidly.

'What the …?' Nick said under his breath and hit the accelerator in an attempt to keep up.

50 mph.

'Yeah, I'm pretty sure that he knows we're following him,' Ruth said dryly.

Nick raised an eyebrow. 'You think?'

The van pulled out onto the opposite side of the road to pass a stationary bus.

Nick swerved out to follow.

60 mph.

'Jesus,' he huffed. 'Where the hell does he think he's going?'

The van took a sharp right.

Nick did the same and the tyres under their 2-litre Astra skidded a little.

The car filled with the thick smell of burnt rubber.

'We'd better put the blues and twos on,' Ruth said as she reached over and hit the button that activated the blue lights embedded in the grill of their car – hence 'blues' – and their twin tone siren – which was the 'twos.'

The loud siren burst into life as they hammered down a side road at 60mph.

The red brake lights of the van burned bright as Kevin Baker slowed the van down almost immediately and pulled it over to the side of the road. It was as if he'd seen the lights and heard the siren and stopped straight away.

'Oh right, now he stops,' Ruth said in a withering tone.

Nick pulled in behind him.

The driver's door opened and a stocky man in overalls got out and looked at them.

'Please don't do a runner,' Nick said. 'I'm not in the mood.'

But the man, who they recognised as Kevin Baker, put out his arms in an innocent gesture and shook his head.

'What's he doing?' Ruth said as she and Nick got out of the car.

'No idea, but he doesn't look like he's going to run or put up a fight which is always a bonus.'

'Kevin Baker?' Ruth asked as they approached and she flashed her warrant card at him.

'Yeah. Look, I didn't know you were coppers,' he said in an almost apologetic tone. 'Sorry.'

'We should arrest you for dangerous driving,' Ruth said.

'You were following me,' Baker said with a shrug. 'I spotted you straight away.'

'Right. And do you often get followed?' Nick asked sarcastically.

'No, but in my old line of work I was trained to spot when I was being tailed and how to take evasive action because it was my life at stake.'

'And you thought your life was at stake just now?'

'No. I suppose it was instinct. Sorry,' he said with an innocent shrug.

Ruth couldn't work out why he was being so incredibly apologetic. Maybe their theory about him being a hitman for hire, and his involvement in Martin Jones' murder was way off.

'What can you tell us about a man called Gary Hastings?' she asked.

Baker frowned and looked utterly baffled. 'Mr Hastings?'

Ruth nodded. 'I take it you know him?'

'Yeah. I'm decorating his mum's house over in Birkenhead. Is that why you've pulled me over?'

'Can you tell us what you were doing in the car park at Broughton Retail Park on the evening of 25th August?'

'Eh?' Baker furrowed his brow. 'I met Mr Hastings and he gave me some money to buy materials and stuff for his mum's job.'

Ruth and Nick looked at each other. Baker seemed pretty convincing.

'Cash in hand?' Nick asked.

Baker hesitated and then gave a guilty nod. 'Jesus, you didn't pull me over because I'm doing some work cash in hand, did you?'

'No,' Ruth sighed.

'I was gonna say,' Baker laughed. 'Otherwise HMRC have really upped their game.'

'Can you tell us where you were on Monday morning between 6am and 9am?' she enquired.

Baker thought for a few seconds. 'I was over working at Mrs Hastings' house. I usually start about 7am. She's an early riser so I like to get cracking.' He pulled out his phone. 'I don't know what all this is about. And I know that some people think that Mr Hastings is a bit dodgy because he runs a scrap yard and that. But I can give Mrs Hastings a ring now and she can tell you I was there if that helps?'

Ruth looked at Nick and shrugged. She was 99% certain that Kevin Baker wasn't a hired assassin. He couldn't have acted or sounded less like one in fact, and it was frustrating.

'Yes, that would be helpful.'

Baker looked on his phone, pressed call, and then put it on speaker.

'Hello?' said the voice of an elderly woman with a Scouse accent.

'Hello Mrs Hastings,' he said. 'It's Kevin Baker here.'

'Oh hello, Kevin. Is everything all right?'

'I'm just talking to some police officers …'

'Oh dear.'

'It's fine. Not a big problem. But they want to know where I was on Monday morning between 6am and 9am.'

'Erm, well you were working over here from about 7am weren't you?'

'That's right. Thanks. I'll be over at yours in about half an hour, okay? Ta ta.'

'Right you are. I'll put the kettle on,' she said as she ended the call.

Ruth rolled her eyes at Nick. *Well that was a ridiculous waste of bloody time.*

Chapter 44

Ruth stood staring at the scene board in frustration. Her eyes roamed around the various suspects, the maps and the photographs.

Nick came over and handed her a fresh coffee. 'Here you go.'

'Ta,' she said without taking her eyes from the board.

He took a sip of his black coffee and peered at the scene board. 'What are you thinking, boss?'

Ruth aired her concerns out loud. 'What if we're barking up the wrong 'proverbial' tree?'

'You mean that Martin's death isn't linked to the robberies, Gary Hastings, or Huw Williams?'

'I just don't know. The more I think about it, the more I think there might be some flaws with that theory.'

Nick raised an eyebrow. 'Such as?'

'From what the NCA and DI Gorski have told us, Gary Hastings is a career criminal who has spent his life surrounded by gangsters. He's into drugs, guns, money laundering, the whole lot.'

'Okay.' Nick turned and gave her a puzzled look. 'I'm still not following you, boss.'

'I've dealt with dozens of professional hits over the years that have involved OCGs and drug gangs,' Ruth clarified. 'It's usually a gunshot and the assassin is gone. Scooter, car. It's over in seconds.'

Nick nodded as if he had now cottoned on to what she was saying. 'But not with Martin Jones.'

'No. The exact opposite actually. He was bludgeoned six times on the head. Then the killer lifted him into a car in broad daylight and set fire to it. And it feels personal.'

'Now you've pointed it out, I agree,' Nick said. 'There was nothing calm or professional about the way Martin was killed.'

'Do we think Huw Williams took it upon himself to shut Martin up?' Ruth asked.

'No, I can't see it. I don't think he has it in him to do that to Martin.'

'Even though he blamed him for Andy Fletcher's death?'

'We interviewed him twice and not once did I ever think that he could be guilty of Martin's murder.'

The doors to the CID office opened and Kennedy and Price walked in with purpose.

'Everything okay?' Ruth asked.

'Martin Jones might have been having an affair with someone,' Kennedy said.

'Who?'

'We're not sure,' Price admitted, 'but he met that person at the Pant-yr-Ochain pub the night before he was murdered.'

Ruth raised an eyebrow. Given what she and Nick had been discussing, it was an interesting development.

'CCTV?' she asked hopefully.

'Yes, but you can't make out the person's face. They're wearing a baseball cap.'

'Can we have a look?' Nick asked.

'Yes, of course.' Kennedy waved a memory stick and headed over to her desk and computer.

Ruth squinted in confusion. 'And we're sure it wasn't Steph Jones?'

Price nodded. 'Yeah. Height and body shape are completely different.'

'But we're certain it's a woman?'

Kennedy pulled a face as she tapped away at her computer and then looked up at the large monitor that was mounted to the wall. 'I think so, but I'm not certain.'

Ruth and Nick turned around to look at the monitor. 'Right, let's have a look.'

Kennedy played the footage from the bar. Ruth could see Martin Jones at the bar and then talking to someone at the table. She saw them holding hands.

'That's definitely a woman,' she stated. 'You can tell by the hands.'

Kennedy pointed to the screen. 'And this is when they start to argue. Eventually Martin storms off but she follows him out to the car park.'

Price fished out his notebook. 'There's CCTV out in the car park, but there was dirt on the camera, so we only got a partial plate. I'm going to ring the DVLA and see if they can help. It's an Audi A3, 19 plate.'

Ruth went over to the monitor to get a good look. 'You might not need to ring the DVLA actually.'

Price frowned. 'Why's that, boss?'

Ruth gestured to the monitor. 'Can you play that back a bit to where they were holding hands across the table?'

Nick's phone rang and he moved away to take the call.

'Yes, boss,' Kennedy said as she shuffled the video back.

'Stop it just there.' Ruth went almost an inch from the screen and looked at the person's hands on the table. 'Now can you use our software to zoom in?'

'Yes, here we go.' Kennedy made the image slightly bigger.

'What is it?' Price asked.

'That's Ruby Allen, Martin's business partner at Headline Properties.'

Price furrowed his brow. 'How do you know that?'

Ruth pointed. 'She's got a fancy silver charm bracelet on her left wrist. It's identical to the one Ruby was wearing when I spoke to her.'

Nick came back and gave Ruth a dark look. 'We've had a 999 call from Huw Williams' wife, Donna. She says she thinks that someone is in their garden.'

'Shit,' Ruth said. 'Where's Huw?'

'He's out doing something in the garage. Daughters are at their grandparents.'

'She's seen someone?' Ruth asked to clarify.

'Yes. She said she saw someone moving through the bushes. She said they were dressed in black and wearing a balaclava.'

'Shit.' Ruth's heart sank. It didn't sound good.

Nick looked at her. 'We can call the tactical firearms en route.'

Ruth turned to Kennedy and Price. 'Right, you two go and ask Ruby why she's hidden her affair with Martin from us.' Then she turned to Nick. 'We'd better get over to Huw's now,' she said with a sense of urgency.

Chapter 45

Ruth and Nick sped down the road towards the Williams' home on the outskirts of Mold. Ruth had contacted uniformed patrols and organised for an armed response vehicle to head to the property as well.

Nick slammed on the brakes and brought the car to a sudden halt outside the small, detached house. They jumped out. Going around to the boot, Ruth and Nick grabbed their Kevlar bulletproof vests and put them on as they jogged towards the front door. Neither the uniformed patrol nor the ARV had arrived yet.

'I just hope we're not too late,' Ruth said with a dark expression.

Donna Williams' call had mentioned an intruder in the back garden. She had also mentioned that Huw had been in the garage, but all Ruth could see was that the up and over door to the garage was open and there was no one inside.

She rang the doorbell and took out her warrant card.

Nothing.

If the family was hiding inside, it wasn't likely that they were going to answer the door.

Nick pointed to what looked like a side alleyway that led to the back of the house.

Ruth nodded and followed him as they went across the front garden, stepped over a small stone wall, and then started to make their way down the side of the house. There were two wheelie bins, a couple of kids' bikes, and a rusty old stepladder which rested against the flank wall.

Spotting that there was a white side door halfway down, Ruth pointed to it.

Nick slowly tried the handle, but the door was locked.

They continued along the alleyway.

The only noise was the sound of their boots on the grey gravel, and the wind that was rocking a nearby wooden fence.

Ruth glanced up. The sky was now a beautiful blue colour with virtually no clouds. There was an aeroplane high above them, its jet engine leaving a white line of vapour that dissected the sky diagonally.

Nick looked at Ruth as they approached the back garden. They moved closer to the flank wall and Nick peered round to check it was safe to continue.

'Looks clear to me,' he whispered.

Where the hell is the ARV? Ruth wondered in frustration. It was meant to be on its way from the coast but that was over half an hour ago. She didn't want to be confronting an armed intruder without back up.

They reached the back garden. It was neat with a lawn, small patio, garden furniture and some children's toys.

Ruth scanned the long row of bushes and hedgerow that ran along the back of it.

Nothing.

'You see anything?' she asked Nick in a soft voice.

He shook his head. 'No, nothing, boss.'

Moving over the lawn, Ruth could hear the distant sound of someone cutting their grass. The air smelled of the nearby lavender plants.

She got to the patio and saw that there were glass patio doors that led inside. They were closed.

As they moved towards the glass, Ruth and Nick cupped their hands to look inside. There were two sofas, a large television, and more children's toys on the cream carpet. Dotted along the wall were family photos in frames.

Inside there was a door open and what looked like a hallway beyond that.

Then Ruth saw something, or someone, move by the door.

What was that?

A head appeared.

It was Huw Williams.

His sudden appearance startled her. 'Bloody hell,' she said under her breath.

Huw made his way into the room. He gestured to the patio doors to indicate that he was going to unlock them and let Ruth and Nick inside.

Ruth nodded to indicate that she understood what he was signalling.

Suddenly, Huw's face completely changed. His eyes widened in fear as he looked past Ruth and Nick and out into the garden.

In the reflection of the glass, Ruth spotted a figure in black running towards them across the lawn from the back of the garden.

Jesus!

Turning around, she saw the figure was dressed all in black and wearing a balaclava.

The figure held up a handgun and pointed it at them.

'No!' Ruth shouted as she and Nick instinctively ducked down and hit the concrete patio.

CRACK! CRACK! CRACK!

Ruth spun around to see three holes in the glass.

Huw stumbled.

There were three dark bullet wounds in his chest and stomach.

He collapsed to the floor.

'No,' Ruth yelled.

As the gunman ran away across the patio, Nick sprinted after him and rugby tackled him to the ground.

They wrestled but the gunman got to his feet.

Nick tried to get up to follow but the gunman punched him in the stomach.

Nick fell backwards and lay on the ground.

Ruth sprinted over.

He was lying on his back, but his eyes were open, and he was gasping for breath.

He was winded.

'Are you all right?' she asked him.

He nodded as he tried to get his breath. 'Yeah, I'm fine.' He sat up on the ground as he continued to take deep breaths. Then he looked at her. 'Go after him. I'll call for the paramedics.'

He tossed Ruth the car keys.

'Seriously, I'll be fine,' he reassured her. 'Go.'

They glanced over at Huw Williams who was lying motionless on the carpet by the patio doors. It didn't look like he was going to need a paramedic.

There was a loud scream from inside as Donna Williams rushed over to her husband.

Ruth saw Nick reach for his Tetra radio.

'Okay,' she said as she broke into a run and sprinted back down the side alleyway to the front of the house.

Getting out to the road, she saw a scooter hurtle around a bend in the road.

The gunman was sitting on the back.

Right, Ruth thought. *I'm not letting you get away.*

She jumped into the car, started the engine and then stamped down on the accelerator. The 2-litre engine roared as she sped away from the curb in the direction that she'd seen the scooter heading.

As Ruth hurtled around the bend, she reached for the seatbelt without taking her eyes off the road, pulled it across her and then clicked it into place.

She reached over and clicked on the internal police radio. As she came around the bend, she saw the scooter and the gunman and rider up ahead.

'Three-six to Control, three-six to Control,' she said urgently into the Tetra radio. 'Are you receiving?'

'Control to three-six, we are receiving, over,' the computer aided dispatch operator said.

'This is DI Ruth Hunter. I am currently in pursuit of suspect and rider on a black scooter. Proceeding at speed, north out of Mold on the B544. I need an ARV asap, over.'

'Three-six, received, stand by. Are you okay, over?'

'Yes, I'm fine. Just. Over.'

Looking up, Ruth could see that the scooter was about a hundred yards ahead. There were cars parked on either side of the road which made it very narrow and meant that she had to slalom in and out at high speed.

Missing a van by what felt like a millimetre, Ruth winced. *I wish Nick was here to do the driving.*

As the road opened up and became less residential, she put her foot down and hit a higher speed. She took the Astra from 60mph up to 70mph.

The scooter was getting closer and closer.

Ruth assumed that the smaller engine on the gunman's scooter would be no match for the 2-litre Astra she was driving.

The Tetra radio crackled. 'Three-six from Alpha Nine. Three-six from Alpha Nine, are you receiving, over?'

Ruth knew that Alpha Nine was the code for the armed response vehicle that had been scrambled from the North Wales Tactical Firearms Unit.

She clicked the grey talk button on the radio that was at the centre of the dashboard. 'Alpha Nine, this is three-six. I am receiving, go ahead, over.'

'Ma'am, we are three miles from target location,' the ARV driver explained. 'Do you still have visual contact on suspect's vehicle? Over.'

Ruth glanced left. 'Yes, I have visual contact. I am currently heading north on the A541.' Then she looked at the GPS that was up on a small screen just above the radio on the dashboard. 'I have just passed a right-hand turn to Blackbrook Road, over.'

'Received, three-six. I can see your current location. Our ETA is seven minutes, over.'

'Received,' Ruth said as she continued to make ground on the scooter. Seven minutes was going to be too long. By her estimation, it was now about 50 yards ahead and she was closing.

Then the scooter took a hard right-hand turn without warning.

'Shit!' Ruth growled as she gripped the steering wheel and spun it hard while applying the brake.

For a moment, she thought she was going to lose control and roll the car.

Whipping the steering wheel back the other way – something she'd seen Nick do in high-speed pursuits – she straightened the car.

According to the GPS map, they were now heading north up the B5121. And at the top of that was the town of Holywell. Maybe that's where they were heading?

Ruth was watching the scooter like a hawk as they hurtled along.

Then she saw the intense red of the scooter's brake lights.

What's he slowing for?

To her dismay, she saw a small gap in the hedgerow and the green sign that signalled a footpath.

'Are you bloody joking?' she growled as she slammed on the brakes and skidded.

As the Astra came to a halt with a squeal of tyres, Ruth saw the scooter whizzing away down the footpath across a field.

There was no way of following it.

'For fuck's sake!' she shouted and hit the steering wheel in frustration.

Chapter 46

Kennedy and Price pulled up on the driveway to Ruby Allen's home and got out. The DVLA had confirmed that Ruby owned a white Audi A3 which Kennedy saw was sitting on the drive. It was the car they had seen in the car park at the Pant-yr-Ochain pub.

Price looked at the detached house and did a little whistle under his breath. 'Nice place.'

'I assume there aren't many houses like this in Prestatyn?' Kennedy said as they walked up the gravel drive towards the front door.

Price gave a look of mock offence. 'Why? What are you trying to say about Prestatyn?'

Kennedy pulled a face. 'Sorry, I just …'

Price grinned. 'I'm joking. There are no houses like this where I grew up.'

'Same here,' Kennedy agreed as she gave an authoritative knock on the door. 'I grew up on the fourth floor of a South London housing estate.'

A few seconds later, the door opened and a young man in his early 20s looked out from under a floppy fringe.

'Hello?' he mumbled incoherently. His eyes were slightly bloodshot, and if Kennedy didn't know better, she would guess that he'd been smoking weed.

She and Price got out their warrant cards. 'DC Kennedy and DC Price, Llancastell CID. Is Ruby Allen in?'

'Yeah,' he mumbled, and opened the door for them to go inside.

'I take it you're her son?' Price asked as they went into the large hallway.

'Oh yeah,' he said very awkwardly. 'I'm Ollie.' Then he pointed up towards the ceiling. 'I'll just go and get her.'

Ollie disappeared down the hallway and up the stairs.

'He's wasted, isn't he?' Price commented.

'Definitely,' Kennedy said as she looked around the hallway.

There was a large photo of Ollie and a man, whom she assumed was his dad, on a golf course. They had their arms around each other, and they were laughing.

Ollie came back with Ruby behind him.

'Oh hi,' she said, sounding confused. 'Has something happened? Is it to do with Martin?' She sounded a little agitated.

'It's just routine. There are a couple of things that we need to clarify with you actually,' Kennedy said. 'If you've got a couple of minutes.'

Ruby furrowed her brow and looked slightly annoyed. 'I've been through everything already.'

Kennedy spotted the charm bracelet on Ruby's wrist. It was the same as the one in the video, and now that she looked at Ruby, she could see that it was definitely her in the video. She gestured to an open door. 'Please, it won't take a minute,' she reassured her.

'Very well,' Ruby said with an irritated sigh as she beckoned for them to follow her into the living room.

Kennedy and Price went over to a large, expensive looking sofa and sat down as Ruby went over to an armchair.

Kennedy watched her. Ruby must have been concerned that they would find out that she'd been having an affair with Martin. She assumed that Ruby's huffy attitude was an attempt to cover her agitation.

Kennedy sat forward on the sofa and looked directly at Ruby who was now fiddling with the bracelet on her wrist. 'We'd like to ask you about the nature of your relationship with Martin.'

Ruby gave them a suspicious look. 'He's my business partner. I don't know what you're getting at?' she said defensively.

'Really?' Kennedy said in a distinctly incredulous tone. She then waited for a few seconds to allow the tension to build. 'I think you do, Ruby.'

Ruby gave a nervous laugh. 'I really have no idea what you're talking about.'

Price crossed his legs as they waited for a few more seconds. It was a very effective tactic. The more time you allowed a suspect to be in their own head, the greater the tension and anxiety. And the more likely they were to break and tell you the truth.

Price took a breath and then said in a steady tone, 'We've seen the CCTV from the Pant-yr-Ochain pub. You met with Martin there the night before he was murdered.'

Ruby's face fell, and then a few seconds later her eyes filled with tears. Her defensive body language wilted away. 'Yes,' she whispered.

'You were having an affair with him?' Kennedy asked, but it wasn't really a question.

'Yes,' Ruby said quietly as she looked away into space.

'How long had you been having an affair for?'

Ruby wiped the tears from her face and took a deep, audible breath to steady herself. 'It was over.'

'The affair had finished?'

'Yes. We met that night to talk, but we ended up arguing. It was horrible.'

'What did you argue about?' Price asked as he started to write some notes in his notebook.

Ruby hesitated in answering.

'You need to tell us what you were arguing about, Ruby,' Kennedy said in a gentle tone that was designed to coax the truth from her.

She nodded, looked away and whispered, 'I wanted us to get back together. I really missed him.' Her eyes filled with tears again and she sniffed.

Price stopped writing and glanced over at her. 'How long had the affair gone on for?'

'About a year.'

'And when did it finish?'

'Two months ago.'

Kennedy frowned. 'Can you tell us why the affair finished?'

'First of all, my husband found out.'

Ruby's answer immediately grabbed Kennedy's attention. The most common cause of murder was love, affairs, and broken relationships.

'Can you tell us your husband's name?'

'Marcus.'

'And how did Marcus react when he found out you and Martin were having an affair?'

Ruby gave an ironic snort. 'He went crazy. He was furious.'

'Violent?'

Ruby looked down at the floor and nodded.

'He hit you?' Kennedy said very gently.

'Yes,' she admitted as she blew out her cheeks. It was all getting too much for her .

'And where is Marcus now?'

'He left me and Ollie, and he flew back to Belfast to live. That's where he's from,' Ruby explained.

'That must have been very difficult.'

'It was. I mean it is. I don't blame him,' she said quietly, 'but Marcus and Ollie were very close. It's been incredibly difficult for Ollie to deal with.'

'I assume that it's them in the photo in the hallway?' Kennedy asked.

'Yes. Marcus taught Ollie to play golf when he was very young. Until Marcus left us, he and Ollie played all the time,' Ruby said quietly.

Kennedy exchanged a look with Price. Marcus Allen clearly had a strong motive for murdering Martin Jones, but he'd not been on their radar until now.

'Do you know if Marcus has been back to this country recently?' Kennedy asked.

Ruby shook her head. 'No. He came back for Ollie's birthday but that was two months ago.' Then Ruby's face fell as she looked at them both. 'Do you think Marcus …?'

Kennedy looked over at Ruby as she processed what they'd been talking about, and the possibility that her husband was somehow involved in Martin's murder.

Price stopped writing and looked over. 'What about Steph Jones? Did she have any idea that you and Martin were having an affair?'

'Yes. That's really why we stopped seeing each other. Steph told Martin that if he finished the affair, she would forgive him, and he could stay in the family home.'

Kennedy glanced at Price. Up until now, Steph Jones

had made no mention of Martin and Ruby's affair. And that was very suspicious.

Chapter 47

Kennedy and Price got out of the car outside Steph Jones' home and made their way up the driveway. Looking up, Kennedy saw the front door opening and Georgie coming out. Despite Steph Jones' request, Georgie was still acting as the temporary family liaison officer until another one could be found.

'Saw you pulling up,' she said as they approached. Then she gave them a quizzical look. 'Something up?'

Kennedy raised an eyebrow knowingly. 'Yeah, you could say that.' She gestured to the house. 'Steph around?'

'It's all right. She's sitting out the back vaping for Wales,' Georgie explained with a wry expression. 'What's going on?'

Price looked at her. 'It seems that Martin and Ruby Allen had an affair for a year.'

Georgie's eyes widened. 'What?'

'It gets worse,' Kennedy said with a knowing look, and then gestured to the house. 'It seems that Steph was fully aware of this. She told Martin if he broke off the relationship, he could stay in the family home.'

'And did he?'

'Apparently,' Kennedy replied.

'But Ruby's husband, Marcus, also found out about the affair,' Price added. 'He was violent towards her, and then moved out of the house and went back to Belfast where he's from originally.'

Georgie raised an eyebrow. 'Do we know if he's back in Wales?'

'Not yet.' Kennedy gestured to the house again. 'We'd better go and see what Steph has to say for herself.'

Georgie nodded as they all headed inside. 'Might explain what's happened between Steph and Lilly then.'

'Maybe,' Kennedy agreed. 'Has Lilly been back?'

Georgie shook her head. 'Not since I confronted Steph about seeing them kiss. My guess is that Steph has told her to stay clear while I'm here.'

'You think Steph could have been involved in Martin's murder?' Price asked as they headed down the hallway.

'Possibly. A woman scorned and all that,' Georgie replied, 'but it's pretty obvious that Lilly and Martin were close as brother and sister. Would Steph do that to Martin given her current relationship with Lilly?'

'Doesn't sound likely,' Price agreed.

They went out of the kitchen door and into the garden.

Kennedy raised an eyebrow. 'Although you only have their word that Lilly and Martin were close.'

'True,' Georgie agreed.

Steph was sitting at the garden table with a blanket around her shoulders. She turned to see them approaching and blew a cloud of vape in the air.

'Has something happened?' she asked, sounding agitated. 'Have you found out who killed Martin?'

'I'm afraid not,' Kennedy said in a gentle voice.

'DC Kennedy and DC Price just want to go through a few things with you, if that's okay?' Georgie explained.

Steph gave them all a withering look and let out a sigh. 'I don't know what else there is to tell you.'

Kennedy pulled out one of the rattan chairs. 'Okay if we sit down?' She wasn't going to wait to be asked to sit down.

Steph nodded and sucked on her vape again.

Georgie made her way back into the house.

Price pulled out his notebook and pen. 'We've just been speaking to Ruby Allen,' he said in a nonchalant tone.

'Okay,' Steph said with a defensive shrug.

Kennedy waited a few seconds and then looked at her. 'We know that Ruby and Martin had an affair.'

Steph pulled a face. 'What?'

Kennedy narrowed her eyes. 'Come on, Steph. There's no point pretending that you didn't know. I understand that it's painful for you to talk about, but we do need to understand why you didn't tell us about this before?'

Steph let out a frustrated sigh. 'Because it was over. It'd been over for a couple of months. I didn't think it was relevant to what had happened to Martin.'

'Really?' Price said, sounding surprised. 'It must have been very upsetting for everyone involved.'

'Of course it was,' Steph snapped.

'What do you know about Marcus Allen?' Kennedy asked.

'Marcus?' she said, in a way that implied she knew him relatively well. 'Why are you asking me about him?'

'We're looking for anyone who had a grudge against Martin. And DI Hunter asked you if you knew anyone who might want to harm him, or if there was anything significant in his life recently that needed to be looked at. How could you not think that their affair wasn't relevant to what happened to him?'

Steph blinked as she looked a little teary. 'I just wanted to believe that it was all over,' she said very quietly. 'I'd tried to put it out of my mind, and I didn't want to talk about it ... Plus I knew that Andy Fletcher's accident and death had been a huge source of worry for Martin. I just assumed that it had something to do with that.'

'That wasn't really your decision to make, was it?' Price said. 'We need to know everything, and then we'll decide what is or isn't relevant.'

Kennedy looked at Price. It was the first time she'd seen him challenge someone like that and she was impressed.

She then looked at Steph. She wasn't sure that she fully believed her. 'Do you have any contact with Marcus Allen?'

'What?' Steph said, furrowing her brow. 'Why would I have any contact with Marcus? We weren't friends. I just met him at a few social events when he was with that woman.'

Steph's answer was a little too quick and angry for Kennedy's liking. It felt as if she was hiding something from them.

'Okay,' Price said, as he scribbled in his notebook. 'So, you've had no contact with Marcus since he left for Belfast. Is that correct?'

'Yes. I don't know why you're concerning yourself with Marcus,' Steph said witheringly. 'He's a gentle giant. He wouldn't harm a fly.'

Kennedy exchanged a look with Price. If what Ruby had told them was true, then Marcus was anything but 'a gentle giant'.

'Did you know that Martin and Ruby had met at the Pant-yr-Ochain pub the night before he was murdered?' Kennedy asked calmly.

'What?' Steph virtually spat out the word. 'No, he wouldn't have done that.' Then she looked crushed and began to cry. 'He said he had a business meeting.' Then she looked at Kennedy as she wiped her tears away. 'Why did they meet? Had they started having an affair again?' she asked, sounding distraught.

'No,' Kennedy reassured her. 'Ruby wanted him back but he told her that wasn't going to happen and that it was over.'

'Really?' Steph looked relieved at what Kennedy had told her. 'You're not just saying that?'

'No. That's what Ruby told us, and we have no reason to think that she was lying to us,' Price said gently.

Steph nodded to herself. 'I don't think I could have beared it if I thought Martin had started to see her again.'

'Yes, that's understandable,' Kennedy said quietly as she and Price got up from where they'd been sitting. 'Obviously we will keep you updated with any developments in our investigation.'

'Okay, thank you,' Steph said in a virtual whisper as they turned and walked away.

As they went into the kitchen, Georgie looked up from where she was sitting at the kitchen table nursing a cup of tea.

'What did you think?' she asked.

Kennedy looked around to make sure that Steph hadn't followed them back down the garden. 'I'm not sure. She said that she didn't mention the affair to us because she thought it was over and it wasn't relevant.'

'But?'

'I'm not sure I'm totally convinced that she was telling

us the truth. Or at least my instinct was that she was hiding something from us.'

Georgie looked up at Price. 'Alfie? What did you think?'

'Same. There was definitely something off about the way she was talking to us.'

Kennedy looked over at some keys hanging from a wooden key holder on the wall of the kitchen. She immediately spotted a Mini key – she had one herself and they were distinctive.

Then something occurred to her. It was a fleeting thought but one worth mentioning.

'Has Steph got a car?' she asked.

'Yeah,' Georgie replied, looking puzzled at Kennedy's sudden interest in Steph's car. 'Why do you ask?'

'A Mini?'

'Yes,' Georgie said, still looking baffled.

Price looked equally bemused.

Kennedy started to remember the car that she had spotted quite by chance on the car park CCTV at the Pant-yr-Ochain. 'A red Mini Clubman?'

'What is it?' Price asked.

Kennedy started to piece things together. 'I think Steph was at the pub the night before Martin was murdered.'

Price pulled a face. 'What? How do you know that?'

'I spotted a red Mini Clubman on the car park CCTV because it's exactly the same model as I've got. I didn't give it a second thought. It had some kind of personalised number plate, but I can't quite remember what it was.'

'I didn't notice if Steph's car had a personalised plate,' Georgie admitted.

Then Kennedy looked at Georgie. 'Do you know where it is?'

'Yes, it's in the garage. I'll show you.'

Georgie got up, and Kennedy and Price followed her across the kitchen to a side door to the outside.

They went out into the side passageway and Georgie went to a door that clearly led to the garage which was separate from the house.

Opening the door, Georgie looked at them. 'It's in here.'

Kennedy walked into the garage which smelled musty and of petrol. Then she walked around to the front and looked at the car's number plate.

Price walked around the other side.

SJ 500

'Yeah, that's it. That's definitely the car I saw,' Kennedy said quietly. 'She must have followed Martin to the pub and seen him and Ruby together.'

Price was cupping his hands and looking through the back window into the boot of the car. Then he turned to them both with a dark expression. 'There's a green petrol can in here.'

'Right,' Kennedy said with a sense of urgency. 'We need to call this in. And we need a forensic team all over this car.'

She marched out of the garage, down the passageway and out into the garden.

Steph turned around at the sound of Kennedy approaching and gave her a bewildered look. 'What are you …'

'Steph Jones,' Kennedy said sternly. 'I'm arresting you on suspicion of the murder of Martin Jones.'

'What?' she cried.

'You do not have to say anything. But anything you do say can be taken down and used in a court of law.'

Steph just frowned at her in utter panic. 'I don't understand.'

'Come on, Steph,' Kennedy said, gesturing for her to stand up. 'I need to take you in.'

Chapter 48

Ruth pressed the button on the recording equipment and said, 'Interview conducted with Stephanie Jones, 3.30pm, Interview Room 1, Llancastell Police Station. Present are Stephanie Jones, Detective Constable Jade Kennedy, Duty Solicitor Karen Symes, and myself, Detective Inspector Ruth Hunter.'

Ruth sat down and looked over at Steph who seemed utterly terrified. She was now wearing a regulation grey sweatshirt and joggers as her clothes had been taken away for forensics. Since arriving, she'd had her fingerprints taken, her fingernails clipped, and a DNA swab.

'Just to remind you, Steph, you are currently under arrest on suspicion of the murder of Martin Jones,' Ruth said. 'Do you understand that?'

'This is ridiculous,' Steph said very quietly. She looked lost and broken. 'I didn't murder my husband.'

Kennedy reached over and took a document from a folder. She turned it for Steph to look at. 'For the purposes of the tape, I am showing the suspect Item Reference 893N. These are notes based on an interview that you gave to DI Hunter and DS Evans on Tuesday. In this interview, you were asked if you knew of anyone who might want to harm Martin or had a grudge against him. You were also asked if there had been anything significant in his life, either personally or professionally, that you felt was relevant. You spoke about the accident in which Andy Fletcher was killed the previous year, and the grievance that his widow Sonia Fletcher had against Martin. Is that correct?'

Steph nodded but looked down at the floor as she bit at the cuticles on her nails. 'Yes.'

'However, you failed to mention that you had discovered that Martin and his business partner, Ruby Allen, had had an affair lasting a year,' Kennedy continued. 'An affair which had only ended two months ago. Is that correct?'

Steph nodded slowly. 'Yes.'

Ruth leaned forward and looked at her. 'Steph, can you see how suspicious that looks to us? You discovered that Martin was having an affair. That gives you a motive to kill him, do you understand that?'

'But I didn't,' Steph stammered. 'I couldn't do that to him.'

'And the fact that you chose not to tell us is very surprising,' Kennedy added.

Silence.

Steph's eyes filled with tears. 'I don't understand how this is happening. My husband has been killed and you're accusing me of doing it. It's just madness.'

'Where were you on Monday morning between 6am and 9am, Steph?' Ruth asked.

'I was in bed asleep until 7am,' she sobbed. Then she wiped the tears from her face. 'Then I got the kids up and dressed, and I dropped them at breakfast club.'

'What time did you drop your children at breakfast club?'

'8am,' she replied with a sniff.

Kennedy narrowed her eyes. 'Can anyone verify that you were there at that time?'

Steph thought for a couple of seconds. 'Yes. Tracy who runs the club.' Steph sounded more confident as she realised that she might have a decent alibi. 'I owed her some money, so I gave her cash, but she didn't have any change so she said she'd give it to me next time.'

'And that was on Monday morning?' Ruth asked. 'We will be checking with her.'

'Yes,' Steph said, sounding desperate. 'I promise you. Just ask her. She'll tell you that I was there at that time.'

Ruth looked over at Kennedy. If Steph's story was true, then it would have been virtually impossible for her to have been over at Heswall at the time that Martin was murdered.

And that meant they might be back to square one again.

Chapter 49

Garrow walked down the corridor of Llancastell University Hospital. Having arrived on the second floor, he was heading towards a ward that was next to the critical care unit where he had discovered Lucy Morgan was. Even though he knew that seeing her and talking to her was a very bad idea, what was the alternative? If he didn't address the problem, he would be looking over his shoulder for the rest of his life, waiting for the next time that she decided to pop up. There was no way he could live like that. Talking to her might not solve the problem. It might actually exacerbate it, but he'd made his mind up and that was that.

Looking up, he spotted the Hamilton Ward and went down the short corridor and in through a set of swing doors. With a quick glance over at the whiteboard, he saw the name Lucy Morgan written in red pen. She was in Room 9. It looked like it was a single room which made his task even easier.

He strode past the nurses' station, looking the other way so that they didn't see his face, and headed along the corridor. A few seconds later he spotted a door with the number 9 on it.

Pushing down on the silver handle, he eased the door open slowly and went inside.

Lucy was lying asleep in bed, her face turned towards the window that looked out over the car park.

Taking a grey plastic chair, Garrow sat down beside the bed. The noise of the chair must have disturbed her as she made a soft groan and then turned her head towards him.

Blinking open her eyes, she squinted at him and then smiled.

'I wondered if you'd come and see me,' she said, and then gave a satisfied sigh.

Garrow scratched his face nervously but didn't say anything for a few seconds.

Maybe this was a really bad idea?

'This isn't that kind of visit actually,' he said resentfully.

'No?' Lucy asked, sounding unfazed by his tone. Then she shifted in the bed, pulled herself up onto the pillows, and stared at him. 'Ah, there you are. Hello.'

'How are you feeling?' he asked with a slight sneer on his face.

'I feel like I've been run over by a car, Jim,' she said with an ironic snort. 'Funny that.'

'It was me.'

She looked at him defiantly. 'What was *you*, Jim?' she asked with a smirk.

'Don't call me Jim,' he snapped, but he knew he couldn't let her weirdness get to him.

Lucy laughed. 'Bit touchy, aren't you? After all, I'm the one who should be a bit touchy when you think about it. I mean you drove your car at me and tried to kill me. Some people might be a bit miffed by that?'

Garrow looked confused. 'You knew it was me?'

'Of course,' she chortled. 'You didn't really think I had amnesia again, did you? I'm becoming quite the expert at playing someone with no memory. But no, I remember everything from the other night very clearly.'

Garrow was slightly thrown by what she'd told him. 'But you chose not to tell anyone?'

'I wouldn't do that to you. Not after everything we've been through together, Jimmy,' she said, shaking her head. 'Did anyone ever call you Jimmy? What did your mother call you?'

'I'm not here to see how you are,' Garrow growled. 'I'm here to tell you that if you come near me again, I'll come after you again. And I will kill you. And I think after the other night, you can see that I'm not joking.'

As the words came out, Garrow instantly regretted his decision to come and see Lucy. His words sounded hollow, even pathetic. Or was that just the horrible self-loathing that had been gnawing away at him in recent days.

Lucy sighed. 'Ahh, poor boy. Well, you don't need to worry. I've met someone. A man. A *real* man. It started on one of those online dating sites. And he wants to whisk me away.'

'What are you talking about?' Garrow asked with disdain.

'I'm being discharged in a day or two and he's coming to pick me up. Then we're moving my stuff out of my house, and I'm going to go and live with him in London. A big penthouse in Chelsea Harbour. So, I don't ever have to see you again.'

Garrow looked at her. He wanted to believe her, but he knew that she was a compulsive liar and a psychopath.

'Well, I'm very pleased for you,' he said sarcastically. 'Goodbye Lucy.' He got up from the chair. 'Just so we're clear, I've explained what I'm going to do if I ever see you again.'

'Yes, you've made that crystal clear,' Lucy said in a withering tone. 'But don't flatter yourself, Jimmy. I have no interest in seeing you.'

Garrow went to the door and left without looking back.

Chapter 50

Georgie was sitting out in Adam's back garden. He had invited her over for an impromptu 'housewarming'. Sitting back, she let the evening sunshine warm her face. Even though it was late August, it was still hot enough to be sitting outside in short sleeves.

'Here we go,' he said as he came out with a tray from the kitchen.

He was wearing a nice blue, short-sleeved shirt, light coloured shorts and fashionable sunglasses.

'Right, sparkling mineral water for the lady,' he said as he put the tray down on the garden table.

'Thanks.' Georgie smiled as she reached over and chinked his bottle of beer with her glass. 'Cheers. Happy housewarming.'

Adam glanced at her apologetically. 'Yeah, I'm sorry you're the sole guest. The only other person I know in North Wales is a paramedic and he's on duty at the moment.'

'Fine by me,' Georgie admitted.

Adam sat back, let out a satisfied sigh, and then sipped from his beer. 'Well, if I'm honest, I'm kind of glad that he's on duty.'

Georgie frowned. *Is he flirting with me?*

Lifting up her sunglasses, she looked over at him with a quizzical smile. 'And why is that, Adam?'

He gave her a cheeky grin. 'Well … I get you all to myself.'

She raised an eyebrow, and felt her pulse quicken. 'Do you now?'

There were a few seconds of silence.

He sat back in his chair and cleared his throat. 'Oh dear, I've just made this a bit awkward, haven't I?'

'Not at all,' she reassured him immediately. 'I like being here. And I like that it's just the two of us.'

He leaned forward and lifted his sunglasses. 'Oh right. Interesting,' he said with a smirk.

Georgie shrugged. 'I hardly know you, but I like you. And I get the feeling that you might like me.'

'Yes, that is definitely true.'

'And I don't know if you like me, *like me*,' she continued, surprised that she was being this candid with someone she was so attracted to, 'but it's irrelevant anyway, isn't it?'

'Erm, explain why it's irrelevant?'

Georgie pointed at her bump.

'That doesn't make it irrelevant,' he said, 'at least not in my book.'

Georgie looked surprised. Was this going way too fast? Probably. Did she care? Not a great deal.

'Really?' she said with more than a hint of suspicion.

Adam nodded. 'Really. Listen, I'm still getting over what happened to me and my last relationship in Manchester. I'm a bit all over the place, but I'd like to spend some time with you and get to know you better ... if you'd like to do that?'

Georgie smiled. 'Yes, I'd very much like to do that.'

Chapter 51

'Right everyone,' Ruth said as she looked out at the assembled CID team. They looked tired, which wasn't surprising. When there was a murder case, most detectives worked very long hours, often only returning home to eat, shower and grab some sleep before heading back in. 'Let's get going on this please. What have we got?'

Price glanced up. 'I've spoken to Border Force and Passport Control. Marcus Allen hasn't entered the country in the past three months. And that covers ferry travel too.'

'Thanks Alfie. Sounds like we can cross him off our list of possible suspects then.'

Kennedy looked over. 'Forensics are confident that they can now get a DNA sample from Martin's shoe.'

'Great. And when do they think they might have it?' Ruth asked hopefully. These days, getting a decent DNA sample from a crime scene was often the key to solving a case.

'First thing tomorrow morning, boss.'

'Of course, there's no guarantee that the DNA is going to get a hit on the national database, or the elimination samples that we took,' Ruth said, thinking out loud to herself. 'Anything on the murder weapon?'

Nick shook his head. 'I spoke to the guys over on The Wirral. Uniformed officers have done an extensive search in the area around the building site. Nothing turned up.'

'And we haven't managed to establish what was used to attack Martin, have we?' Ruth asked, remembering how Amis had described the weapon as being something blunt that left wounds about five inches long.

The team didn't have a response. No one quite knew what they were looking for.

'CID on The Wirral are still looking at the possibility that Martin was killed by a hitman hired by Gary Hastings,' Nick added, 'but they don't have any leads on that.'

'Okay,' Ruth said thoughtfully. 'Because of the way that he was killed, I'm starting to doubt that it was a professional hit.'

Price put his pen up to indicate he wanted to speak. 'No irregularities in any of Martin's bank accounts. I also checked with Companies House. The same is true of Headline Properties. There are no financial worries anywhere.'

'Thanks Alfie.' Ruth turned to look at the scene board. 'Do we think that Steph Jones did this? Jade? What did you think about the interview we conducted with her yesterday?'

Kennedy took a few seconds and then said, 'If I'm honest, I don't believe she is capable of murdering Martin. And I don't think anything in the interview from yesterday changed my mind. Steph has told us a pack of lies from day one. She did follow Martin and see him with Ruby the night before he was murdered, but I checked with the breakfast club at the local school. She was there, bang on 8am with her kids. Logistically there's no way she could have been in Heswall at the time of the murder. And on top of that, I don't think she's got it in her.'

Ruth nodded in agreement. 'Feels like we're a bit stuck at the moment.'

Price, who had just answered an office phone, looked over at Ruth with a sense of urgency. 'Boss?'

'Yes, Alfie?'

'Urgent message from DI Gorski. She's sent a video via email. She wants you to watch it and then call her asap.'

'Is the email on our shared area?'

'I'll take a look,' Kennedy said as she went over to her computer. She started to tap some keys. 'Yes, boss. It's just arrived in there.'

Ruth pointed to the monitor up on the wall. 'Can you play the video on that so we can all see what DI Gorski has sent over?'

'No problem. The email says that it's dashcam from a bus travelling on The Wirral at 6.09am on Monday morning.'

'Okay.' Ruth wondered what they were about to see.

The dashcam footage came up on the wall monitor.

Kennedy pressed play. The image was a little blurry and disorientating, but Ruth could see that the bus was travelling north to south along the road that passed by the Headline Properties development site.

She took a few steps nearer to the screen as the bus got closer to the main gates.

A large car was indicating left, then pulled off the main road and disappeared into the site.

'Sorry, I didn't see that properly. Can you play it again and pause it on the car that is turning left into the site?'

'Yes, boss.'

Kennedy played the footage again and paused when it showed the car.

Ruth went closer to the screen and saw a brand-new white Porsche Cayenne.

She turned to look at Nick.

'Ruby Allen,' they both said in unison.

'Let's go and pick her up.'

Chapter 52

Ruth pressed the button on the recording equipment and said, 'Interview conducted with Ruby Allen, 11.30am, Interview Room 1, Llancastell Police Station. Present are Ruby Allen, Detective Sergeant Nick Evans, Duty Solicitor Bradley Hart, and myself, Detective Inspector Ruth Hunter.'

Ruby folded her arms and looked down at the floor. She hadn't said anything since they'd arrested her two hours earlier at her home.

'Ruby,' Ruth said calmly, 'I'm just going to remind you that you are under arrest and we're recording this interview. Do you understand that?'

'Yes,' she answered in a whisper that was barely audible.

Ruth reached for her laptop and pulled it towards her. 'For the purposes of the recording, I'm going to show the suspect Item Reference 935N.' She clicked on the file footage from the bus, turned the laptop to show Ruby, and played it. 'This is a dashcam taken from a number 34 bus on The Wirral. It was taken at 6.09am on Monday morning.'

Ruby raised her head slowly and looked at the screen.

When the footage showed the Porsche Cayenne turning into the site, Ruth paused it.

'Ruby, this dashcam shows your car pulling into the Headline development site at 6.09am. We think this is roughly 30 minutes before Martin Jones was murdered. Is there anything you'd like to tell us about that?'

Ruby just stared blankly at the screen.

'Ruby,' Nick said. 'Is that your car?'

Ruby nodded. 'Yes. It was me.'

'You arrived at the development site at 6.09am, is that correct?' Ruth asked.

'Yes.'

'Can you tell us why?'

Ruby closed her eyes for a few seconds. 'I went to meet Martin there.'

'Can you tell us why you went to meet Martin there?'

Ruby took a deep breath to steady herself. 'Martin and I had been meeting at the site every morning for weeks.'

Ruth raised an eyebrow. 'Why were you doing that?'

'Why do you think?' she snorted. 'Use your imagination. We had sex in his office there.'

'So, you met him that morning to have sex in his office?' Nick asked to clarify.

'Yes.'

Ruth frowned. 'But you told us that at the Pant-yr-Ochain pub the night before, Martin had made it very clear that your affair was over. That's why you argued.'

'Yes,' Ruby said, 'but I sent him a series of texts on Monday morning begging him to meet up one more time and then I'd leave him alone.'

'Okay,' Nick said. 'So, he agreed to meet you there as you had done many times before. Is that correct?'

'Yes.'

Ruth narrowed her eyes. 'What happened?'

Ruby was staring into space. 'I … I just killed him,' she whispered. Then she looked at them. 'I didn't want anyone else to have him. So, I waited for him, and then I attacked him.'

'What did you use to attack him with?' Ruth asked.

'I can't really remember.' Ruby's eyes filled with tears. 'I just grabbed some kind of tool that was lying around and hit him across the head a few times.'

'What kind of tool was it?'

'I don't know.'

'What did you do with it?'

'I can't remember. I must have just dropped it somewhere.'

'And then what did you do?'

'He was lying there with all this blood,' she sobbed. 'I just didn't know what else to do. I couldn't leave him just lying like that. I dragged him over to his car and put him on the back seat.' Ruby could hardly get her breath now as she tried to explain what she'd done.

'It's okay, Ruby,' Ruth reassured her. 'Just take your time. What did you do next?'

'Then I got some petrol from the storeroom on the site. I poured it into the car, and I set it alight,' she whimpered.

'Can you tell us why you did that?'

She shook her head. 'I don't know. I really don't know. I think after I'd attacked Martin, I just panicked.'

Silence.

Ruth looked over at Nick and then at Ruby. 'Ruby Allen, I'm charging you with the murder of Martin Jones.'

Chapter 53

Two hours later, Ruth was back in CID in front of the assembled team. There was a palpable sense of relief that Ruby Allen had confessed to Martin Jones' murder. The room was full of chatter and the odd laughter.

'Okay, guys, let's settle down now,' Ruth said as she looked out at them. 'We got the result we wanted. And we've got justice for Martin Jones and his family. Ruby Allen will be going away for a very long time for what she did, and I want to thank you for all your hard work on this.'

Nick looked over and smiled. 'And the fact that Ruby Allen has made a full signed confession means that we're not going to trial.'

There was a ripple of chatter. No one in CID looked forward to something like a murder trial. The amount of paperwork that needed to be prepared for the Crown Prosecution Service was vast. Every interview and piece of evidence needed to be checked, then double and triple checked. The other challenging thing about a murder trial was the long period of time that CID officers had to wait before it started. Sometimes up to a year. Often, the facts had long disappeared from their memories as more cases arrived. Having to trawl back through evidence and statements a year later was a monumental pain in the arse.

Ruth held up her hand. 'So, my suggestion is that we have an …'

There were some jeers and boos.

'Hold on, hold on,' she said, grinning, '… early night. Leave here at 5pm and I'll be buying drinks down at The King's Arms.'

There were cheers and a round of applause as Ruth shook her head in amusement and walked back to her office.

She spotted Georgie over by her desk and headed over. 'Hey. I know you're not drinking, but are you coming to the pub later to celebrate?'

Georgie gave her a half smile. 'Do you mind if I don't?'

Ruth looked confused. 'Not even for half an hour?'

'Actually … I'm going on a date,' Georgie confessed in a virtual whisper.

'A date? Wow. Great,' Ruth said, trying not to sound too surprised. 'Who's the lucky guy?'

'His name is Adam. He's a paramedic from Manchester and he's just moved in next door,' she said with a beaming smile. '<u>And</u> he's very attractive.'

'Is he now?' Ruth laughed. 'Well, at the risk of sounding like your mother, be careful and, you know, take your time.'

Georgie smiled. 'Thank you. And for the record, I actually like it when you sound like my mother.'

54

Two days later

It had been an hour since Garrow had parked up opposite Lucy Morgan's house in Acton in Wrexham. Having made a series of calls, he had learned that she had been discharged from Llancastell Hospital that afternoon.

When Garrow arrived in Acton, he had seen that there was a small transit van parked outside the house. And then he had watched a man, who he assumed was Lucy's new 'boyfriend', ferry boxes and small bits of furniture and pack them inside the van. For once, Lucy had been true to her word. She was definitely moving out and there was a new man in her life. His name was Jasper. Garrow had heard her calling to him at one point when she appeared in the doorway.

Jasper looked like he was in his early 50s, so he was significantly older than Lucy. Maybe she needed some kind of father figure. His clothes, and the brand-new Mercedes C-Class that was parked in front of the van, marked him out as being wealthy. Garrow guessed he was some kind of city lawyer or worked in finance. He had that sort of look and manner about him.

Garrow had no idea what Lucy was planning to do with Jasper and her new life in London. There was part of him that wanted to go across the road and warn the utterly oblivious Jasper what he was letting himself in for. What if Garrow turned on the news one night to see Jasper's face and a report that he'd been horribly murdered? Didn't he owe it to him to go over and fill in Lucy's dark back story before his life was ruined?

However, there was another selfish part of Garrow that just wanted Lucy out of North Wales permanently. And if Jasper wanted to whisk her away to London, then more fool him.

Pulling down the car's sun visor, Garrow looked at his reflection in the small mirror. He looked better. For starters, he hadn't had an alcoholic drink for over 72 hours and he was pretty sure that he was now fully detoxed. It was frightening how quickly alcohol had taken him over, and he'd had a brief glimpse of how alcoholism could develop.

He had also finally returned to work. Ruth and Nick had covered for him, and no one else in the CID team knew where he'd been or the depths to which he'd sunk. He was so grateful to them for their support. And he made a promise that he'd never let himself or his colleagues down ever again.

Pushing the sun visor back up, Garrow spotted Jasper closing the doors to the transit with a satisfied slam. Lucy had come out and they had kissed before walking back into her house holding hands.

Garrow let out a sigh of relief. *Thank God for that.*

Turning on the ignition, he pulled slowly away from the curb and prayed that would be the last time that he ever laid eyes on Lucy Morgan.

Chapter 55

Georgie and Adam were sitting in his car on the drive. They'd been to the cinema and had food in Llancastell which was technically their second date in three days.

'Home sweet home,' he said as he turned off the car engine.

'I can't remember the last time I went on a date with a boy to the cinema,' Georgie admitted.

Adam laughed. 'A boy? I guess I'll take that as a compliment.'

Georgie gave him a playful hit on the arm. 'You know what I mean.'

'The first ever date I went on was to the cinema. Rachel Palmer. I was fourteen and completely terrified,' he said. 'I'd been to see the film *Bruce Almighty* with my family the week before, but Rachel said she wanted to see it. So, I went again and tried to show off by predicting what was going to happen in the film because I'd already seen it.'

Georgie chortled. 'And was she impressed?'

'No, I think she found me very annoying.' Adam laughed. 'Then we got a McDonald's and went to sit in the park, but I didn't have the bottle to try and kiss her. I just walked her home.'

'No second date then?'

'No. I called a couple of times, but she never got back to me. The next time I saw her she was outside a pub in town kissing Alex Taylor from the year above. I was gutted.'

Georgie grinned and put her hand on his arm. 'Oh dear. Never mind.'

He shrugged. 'It's all right. Alex Taylor got nicked for drug dealing a few years later, and Rachel has now got three kids.'

Georgie looked over at Adam and their eyes met.

'How is your 'bottle' now?' she asked him.

'I'm not sure. Why are you asking?'

'I thought you might want to kiss me.' Georgie's pulse quickened. She was certain that he did, but what if she'd got it completely wrong?

'I do want to kiss you, but I'm feeling very nervous about making the first move.'

'Oh right,' she said. 'Well, why don't I save you the trouble?'

She leaned in and kissed him on the mouth. Soft at first and then more passionately.

Then she moved back and looked at him.

'We're going to take this nice and slowly, if that's okay?' she said quietly as she felt the butterflies in her stomach.

'That's more than fine by me,' he replied with a beaming smile.

'Why are we sitting in the car when we've both got far more comfortable homes just there?' she asked with a bemused look.

Adam shrugged. 'I suppose it's what people do in films after they've been on a date.'

'Only if the boy is dropping the girl home,' Georgie said, 'except my home is next to yours.'

'True. So, we could get out.'

They laughed at the same time.

Georgie grinned as they opened the car doors and got out onto the drive.

'What are you doing on Saturday?' she asked.

'I've got the day off. I suppose I'll be unpacking more boxes.'

'There's someone I'd like you to meet.'

'Yeah, of course.' Adam moved slowly towards her. Then he leaned in and kissed her on the mouth again. 'Night, Georgie.'

'Night, Adam,' she said as she turned and headed over to her front door.

Chapter 56

The following morning, Ruth and Nick had driven over to the Headline Properties development site to meet DI Gorski. There were a few things to wrap up, and Ruth wanted to thank Gorski for all the cooperation and support that she and The Wirral CID team had given them during the investigation.

As Ruth got out of the car, there was a distinct chill in the air. She wished she'd brought a coat. As she buttoned up her jacket, she could tell that summer was definitely on its way out and autumn was just around the corner. She didn't know what it was, but autumn had such a different light and atmosphere when it did arrive.

Looking over at the bustling site, she could see that there were various workmen, diggers and concrete mixers. The air smelled of diesel from the engines and also the thick smell of wet concrete.

A couple of detectives from Wirral CID were talking to workmen and taking statements. Ruth assumed that there were still people who worked for Headline who needed to give statements about Ruby Allen and possibly her relationship with Martin Jones.

A figure approached.

It was Gorski. She gave them a relieved smile.

'Well done on getting the result we wanted,' she said as she shook their hands.

'Couldn't have done it without your help, Karolina,' Ruth said warmly.

Gorski nodded. 'And a full confession?'

Nick sighed gratefully. 'Saves everyone the pain of a trial.'

Gorski smiled. 'I'm not going to complain about that. I've got enough paperwork to sink a ship, not that we get any gratitude for it,' she groaned.

'Well, if you're ever looking for a change of scene, we're always on the lookout for great DIs in North Wales,' Ruth said, picking up on her disgruntled tone.

'Thanks, I'll bear it in mind,' Gorski said, looking flattered. 'I hear you've already poached an officer from this side of the border?'

'DC Kennedy? Yes, she's been a great addition.'

Nick gave Gorski a quizzical look. 'How did you know that?'

She laughed. 'I'm a detective.'

'Any developments with the case against Gary Hastings?' Ruth asked.

Gorski shook her head in frustration. 'Unfortunately, men like Gary Hastings are Teflon when it comes to stuff like that.'

Before they could continue, there was the sound of shouting from over by a lorry that had a rotating concrete mixer on its back.

Ruth frowned and looked over.

One of the detectives marched over, signalling to

Gorski. 'Workmen have found something hidden under the rubble of the foundations.'

'Okay.' She gestured for Ruth and Nick to follow her.

Ruth had no idea what they had found but it must be significant by the tone of the detective.

As they approached, a couple of workmen were looking into a deep hole which Ruth guessed was for the foundations of a new house. By the looks of it, the concrete mixer was about to pour concrete into the hole.

Peering down into the hole, she saw something long and metallic gleaming in the light.

It was a golf club.

She shared a look with Nick. *What the … ?*

Gorski put her blue forensic gloves on, jumped down into the hole, and retrieved the golf club from where it had been lying.

She came over to them, holding the club with two fingers.

'Could this be the murder weapon?' she asked rhetorically as they peered at the long steel shaft.

Ruth nodded. 'Ruby Allen's son has golf clubs in the house. We saw him playing. Maybe she just grabbed one of them on her way out.'

As Gorski carefully moved some of the dirt and gravel from the head end, they could all see what was underneath.

Dried blood that had some matted hair stuck to it.

'Looks like our murder weapon,' Nick said.

'I'll get prints taken off it to be on the safe side,' Gorski said, 'and we'll do the usual DNA testing on the blood and hair. My guess is that we'll find Ruby Allen's prints all over this, and Martin's DNA.'

'Sounds likely,' Ruth agreed.

'If Ruby hadn't given us a full confession,' Nick said,

'this would have been a vital piece of evidence. But now it'll just be something that supports what she's told us.'

Ruth wasn't listening properly. Something had occurred to her that didn't sit quite right.

She looked at them. 'The strange thing is, when we interviewed Ruby yesterday, I asked her what she had used to attack Martin with. She gave us a vague answer and said that she had just grabbed a tool of some kind that was lying around.'

Gorski looked puzzled. 'Really?'

Nick nodded. 'We asked her what it was, and she said she didn't know. And then we asked what she had done with it, and she said that she had just dropped it somewhere.'

Gorski looked confused and gestured to the golf club. 'And given that we've just found this, none of that makes any sense, does it?'

Ruth narrowed her eyes as she got a sinking feeling. 'No. It really doesn't.'

Chapter 57

By the time Ruth and Nick arrived back at Llancastell CID, they now had huge doubts about the validity of Ruby Allen's confession. Her failure to remember that she had attacked Martin with a golf club seemed very unlikely. And if she didn't attack him with a golf club, who did? There seemed to be only one possibility and that was Ollie Allen. Maybe Ruby had confessed to the murder to save her son.

As they got out of the car in the car park, Ruth got a phone call. It was Georgie.

'Hi Georgie,' she said as she closed the car door. 'We've just arrived back so I'll be in CID in ten minutes. We've got another development.'

'Actually, it's urgent,' Georgie explained. 'I've just taken a call from forensics. They've found a match for the DNA on Martin's shoe and they want to show you.'

'Okay, thanks Georgie. We'll head over there now.'

Ruth ended the call and looked over at Nick. 'Forensics want to show us something and it's urgent.'

Two minutes later, they entered the forensic wing of Llancastell nick and headed for the lab to their left. It was brightly illuminated with several rows of forensic equipment – microscopes, fume hoods, chromatographs and spectrometers – as well as vials and test tubes of brightly coloured liquids.

A lab technician in a full forensic suit, mask, and gloves approached them at the doorway. 'Can I help?' he asked.

'DI Hunter and DS Evans. I've just had a call that you've found something in a DNA sample?'

'Yes,' he nodded, as he handed them forensic gloves and masks to put on. 'I'll take you over.'

They followed him over to see the chief lab technician, Kristin Ryan, whom Ruth had met a few times since arriving in North Wales.

'Hi there. DI Hunter, isn't it?' Kristin asked from behind her mask. She was holding a test tube and looking at a computer screen with a coloured graph on it.

'Yes, that's right. What have you got for us?'

'We've got the trace DNA that we managed to take from Martin Jones' shoe,' she explained. 'After several attempts, we've now managed to get a DNA profile that we can use.'

Ruth exchanged a look with Nick. It was very good news.

'Great,' Ruth said, sounding encouraged. 'And?'

'Well, there's good news and bad news.'

'And the bad news is?' Nick asked.

'We've run the DNA against the national database and there are no hits I'm afraid.'

Ruth felt a little disappointed that there hadn't been a hit. 'And the good news?'

Kristin turned and pointed to a large computer screen that showed the image of the DNA profile. 'So, this is the DNA profile of the sample we obtained from Martin's shoe. It's virtually complete. We usually base our profile on twenty-four genetic markers, each of which contains what we call an STR, a "short tandem repeat". It's basically a section of the DNA that repeats itself.'

Ruth couldn't help but feel a little confused. She looked at Nick who seemed equally baffled.

Kristin looked at them both and said, 'Bear with me, because this is the bit where it gets interesting.' She pointed to the screen. 'So, most markers show two peaks, which you can see here, and these markers produce a unique series of forty-eight numbers. In this instance, we were only able to establish thirty-six numbers, which is pretty good given what we were working with.' She clicked a button and another DNA profile appeared on the screen. 'This is one of the elimination DNA samples that we took from Martin's close family and work colleagues.' She pointed at the screen. 'Here you can see the same patterns.'

Ruth peered closely at the screen. 'Is it me, or do these profiles look exactly the same?'

'Well, nearly,' Kristen said. 'So, this image is the DNA we took from Martin's shoe and then placed over the DNA from one of your elimination samples.' She pointed at the screen again. 'You can see how the peaks are virtually identical.'

Nick raised an eyebrow. 'But not entirely identical?'

'No,' Kristen said. 'It's what we call familial DNA.'

Ruth nodded. She knew what that was. 'So, it could be a parent or a child?'

'Correct.'

'And you're going to tell us that the original elimination DNA sample came from Ruby Allen?'

Kristen frowned. 'Spot on.'

Nick looked at Ruth and nodded. 'Ollie.'

Chapter 58

Ruth and Nick arrived at the Allen's home and pulled up on the driveway. As soon as Ruth got out of the car, she heard the *thwack* sound that they'd heard the first time they visited the house.

That meant that Ollie was playing golf in the garden.

They walked up the drive, down the stone path, and onto the neatly trimmed lawn.

Ollie chipped a golf ball up into the air and then turned to see them. For a second, his expression was calm. But then something about the way they were approaching seemed to spook him.

'Ollie,' Ruth said in a serious tone, 'we're going to need you to come to the station with us.'

He took two steps back and frowned. 'What for?'

Nick walked slowly towards him. 'Come on, Ollie, let's not make this any more difficult than it needs to be, eh?' he said in a composed manner.

'I'm not going anywhere,' Ollie snorted arrogantly. 'You need to talk to my mum or my dad before you can take me with you.'

Ruth shook her head. 'You're over eighteen, Ollie. Your parents have nothing to do with this.' Then she gave him a stony look. 'We found your golf club in the foundations of a house at the Heswall site.'

'So what?' he sneered. 'That doesn't prove anything.' His body language was now nervous and twitchy as he gripped the golf club in his hands.

'We've got your DNA at the crime scene, Ollie,' Nick said, taking another step forward. 'You've got to come with us. It's over.'

Ollie immediately swung the club at Nick. 'You're not taking me. No way.'

Nick moved back to avoid being hit. 'Don't be an idiot. Just put the club down.'

'No chance,' he snapped as he swung it again.

Nick moved forward quickly, putting his hands up to defend himself.

Ollie swung the club, but Nick managed to duck and it flew harmlessly over his head.

However, Ollie continued his swing and brought the club back so that it smashed into Nick's knee.

'Ah,' Nick cried in pain. He clutched his knee and then lost his balance and crumpled to the lawn. 'Jesus!'

Ollie threw the club at Ruth and then turned and ran off.

'You okay?' she asked Nick as she went to him.

'Not really,' he groaned, 'but I'll live.'

Ruth raced across the lawn after Ollie who was now at a small wooden fence which separated the garden from fields.

He climbed over and continued to run.

With her arms pumping, Ruth broke into a steady jog, cursing her lack of fitness. Within seconds she was gasping for breath.

Ollie darted left, heading for a steep hill.

To the right, barbed wire and an aluminium fence marked out a field where sheep were grazing. A couple of them looked at Ruth with disinterest as she sprinted past.

Ollie was now fifty yards away.

Ruth was running flat out, and her shoes were beginning to rub against her heels. With the back of her hand, she wiped the sweat from her forehead.

Seventy yards.

Bloody hell!

Ollie glanced back at her anxiously and then slipped and fell.

'Stay there!' Ruth yelled. 'Ollie!'

Ollie got to his feet, but he had clearly twisted his ankle.

He began to hobble and hop away.

'Ollie, just stop there!' she gasped. 'You're not going anywhere.'

He was now only thirty yards away.

He turned, stumbled, and fell to the ground again.

A few seconds later, Ruth was on him. She grabbed her cuffs, pulled his hands behind his back and cuffed him.

'Oliver Allen …' She puffed out a laboured breath. 'I'm arresting you for the murder of Martin Jones. You do not have to say anything, but anything you do say can be used in a court of law.'

Chapter 59

An hour later, Ruth pressed the button on the recording equipment and said, 'Interview conducted with Oliver Allen, 12.30pm, Interview Room 2, Llancastell Police Station. Present are Oliver Allen, Detective Sergeant Nick Evans, Duty Solicitor Bradley Michaels, and myself, Detective Inspector Ruth Hunter.'

Ollie sat with his head in his hands. He had spent most of the journey back to Llancastell crying and shaking his head.

'Okay, Ollie,' Ruth said gently. 'I'm going to need you to tell us what happened on Monday morning at the Headline Properties site in Heswall.'

Ollie stared at the floor as if he hadn't heard what she'd said.

'Ollie?'

He looked up and seemed confused.

'You need to tell us about what happened on Monday morning in Heswall,' she repeated calmly.

He took a few seconds to compose himself. Then he looked at the duty solicitor who gave him a reassuring nod.

'I drove over to the site in Mum's car,' he mumbled. 'It was very early.'

'How did you know Martin was going to be there?' Nick asked.

'I took my mum's phone while she was sleeping and sent him some texts asking him to meet her there asap,' he explained. 'I said it was urgent. He sent a message back to say that he'd be there.'

Ruth frowned. 'And your mum didn't see those messages?'

Ollie shook his head. 'No. I deleted them,' he explained, as if that was obvious.

Ruth leaned forward and looked directly at him. 'Ollie, I'm going to need you to tell us why you arranged to meet Martin at the Heswall site.'

He closed his eyes and shook his head very slowly. 'I wanted to kill him,' he whispered.

'Why did you want to kill him?' Ruth asked in a quiet voice.

Ollie looked at her. His face twisted with anger. 'He was the reason why my dad left us and moved away. I never get to see him anymore.'

'You blamed Martin for the affair with your mum?'

'Yes, of course,' he said with a slight sneer. 'I know what Martin's like. He'd been after my mum for years.'

Ruth narrowed her eyes. 'And how do you know that?'

'I heard my mum and dad rowing when the affair all came out. My dad said he'd always suspected that there was something going on. Then Dad actually blamed himself for the affair because he's away on business a lot.'

Ruth nodded and paused for a second. 'And you didn't blame your mum for what happened?'

'I did,' he said uncertainly. 'Just not as much as Martin.'

Nick scratched his beard and said, 'And why was that?'

Ollie furrowed his brow. 'I don't know. I just did.'

'So, that morning, you sent Martin messages to meet you in Heswall,' Ruth stated. 'Did you take a golf club or was that already in the car?'

'No, I took it.'

Nick looked over. 'Why did you take it?'

Ollie pulled a face as if to say, *Why do you think I took it?* 'To attack him with.'

'Right.' Ruth was slightly taken aback at the callous way Ollie had described this. 'You got to the site before Martin arrived?'

'Yes. I had a hood and a bally on, and I hid in one of the houses. When Martin arrived, I just came out and started to hit him with the club.'

'And your intention was to kill him?' Nick asked.

'Yeah, I think so.'

Ruth looked at him. 'You think so?'

'I mean, yes.' Ollie suddenly looked overwhelmed by emotion. 'I just wanted him to be dead so my dad could come back and live with us.'

'And once you'd attacked Martin, what did you do then?'

Ollie blinked as he tried to get his breath and tears welled in his eyes. 'I lifted him into the car. And then I torched it.'

'Where did you get the petrol from?'

'They keep cans of petrol for all the machines,' Ollie explained as he composed himself again.

Nick frowned. 'Was it your intention to burn the car with Martin inside when you first arrived?'

'Yeah,' he said quietly. 'I'd seen it on a TV series. They said there'd be no forensics if you did that. I didn't think I'd get caught.'

'And what about the golf club?'

He shrugged. 'I hid it under the rubble in the foundations of one of the houses. I just assumed that they'd concrete it over and the club would be gone forever.'

Ruth sat back for a few seconds and then looked at Nick. They had more than enough now to formally charge Ollie with Martin's murder.

'Okay, Ollie. You will be charged today with Martin Jones' murder,' Ruth explained, 'and you'll be placed on remand until you appear before a Crown Court where you will have a plea hearing.'

Ollie's face was red and blotchy from where he'd been crying. 'Can I see my mum?'

Ruth nodded. 'I'll see what I can do,' she said as she and Nick got up from the interview table.

'What's going to happen to her? She was just trying to protect me.'

'As you've confessed to Martin's murder, your mother will be facing lesser but still very serious charges of aiding and abetting an offender and obstructing a murder investigation.'

'Will she go to prison?' he asked.

'Yes. She will definitely go to prison.'

He looked crushed. 'How long for?'

Ruth shook her head. 'I can't tell you that. It'll be up to the judge to decide.

Ollie looked like he was going to be sick. 'She didn't do anything.'

Ruth looked at Ollie. He looked gobsmacked by what she had told him.

Ruth and Nick turned away and headed for the door.

Chapter 60

Ruth was scurrying around her kitchen, tidying and making sure drinks were chilling and snacks were in the appropriate bowls. She glanced at her watch. It was 2.05pm. Nick, Amanda and Megan were out in the garden with Sarah, Daniel, and Ruth's daughter Ella.

The sunlight streamed through the kitchen window and glistened on the sink and taps. Even though it was the end of the summer, they had lucked out with the weather. It was warm enough to wear a t-shirt. Ruth wasn't sure if it was the right time of year to be able to call it an 'Indian Summer' or not. She wasn't quite sure why it was called that in the first place, but she knew that it was such a bonus to be able to have everyone outside.

Ella popped her head through the door that led out to the garden. 'Do you need a hand with anything?'

Ruth gave her a wry smile. 'Well, you've timed that well.'

'Actually, I made sure that you'd completely finished everything before I came in and offered,' she joked.

Ruth rolled her eyes. 'Funny.'

Daniel squeezed past Ella and looked at Ruth. 'Can I have some crisps please?'

'How many packs have you had today?' she asked him, raising an eyebrow.

'Erm, one,' he said with an innocent shrug.

'You do know that there's lots of salt *and* sugar in crisps?' she asked.

He gave her an exasperated nod of the head. 'Erm, yes. That's why they taste so nice.'

Ruth tried to sound stern but failed miserably. 'Okay, one more pack but no more after that.'

Daniel grabbed a packet of crisps from the work surface and disappeared back out of the door.

'You look like you could do with a drink,' Ella said as Sarah came into the kitchen from the hallway.

'A glass of rosé, thanks,' Ruth said with an amused look. She didn't know if Ella was offering, but she didn't care. She looked at her watch again. 'Where are they?'

Ruth was referring to Georgie and Adam. She was feeling a little apprehensive about meeting the new man in Georgie's life. Call it her maternal instinct, but Georgie was soon to be a single parent and she didn't need to be messed around. Plus, the last person she got involved with had nearly cost her her life.

'Hey, take it easy,' Sarah said, giving Ruth a kiss and putting a comforting hand on her shoulder.

Ella shot Ruth a look. 'And be nice to him.'

Ruth widened her eyes indignantly. 'I don't know what you mean,' she protested with a knowing smile.

Sarah and Ella laughed.

'Yeah, okay,' Ella groaned. 'I, more than anyone else on the planet, should know how protective you can be.'

'I don't think it's a bad thing to feel protective of the people I love,' Ruth pointed out.

Sarah pulled a face. 'Yeah, but we don't want to scare him off either.'

Ruth shrugged. 'If he gets scared off by me giving him a bit of a grilling, he doesn't deserve to be with Georgie.'

'Mum!' Ella remonstrated.

The doorbell went.

'Oh, right, that will be them,' Ruth said, straightening her hair as she went down the hallway to the front door. She opened it with her best smile.

Georgie was standing next to a tall, handsome man with sandy hair.

'Hi,' Ruth said in an overly-friendly tone. 'You must be Adam.'

Adam reached out to shake her hand. 'Nice to meet you.' In his other hand he had a beautiful bunch of flowers. 'These are for you,' he said, handing them over.

'Oh, how lovely.' Ruth was already thinking that he was making a very good impression. 'You can come again,' she joked. 'Come in, come in.'

They came into the hallway.

Adam gestured to his feet. 'Do you want me to take off my shoes?'

'No, no. No need.'

'What a lovely home you have,' he said, looking around as they came into the kitchen.

'Adam is still living out of boxes,' Georgie said.

He nodded. 'I'm just waiting for the time to build some shelving units.'

Ruth shot a look over at Ella and Sarah, and raised an approving eyebrow.

'Except I dragged him over here today,' Georgie quipped.

Ruth gestured to the fridge. 'Can I get you guys drinks? Beer, Adam?'

Adam held up his hand. 'I'm driving, but a sparkling water would be great.'

Georgie nodded. 'Same please.'

Ruth gestured to the door leading outside. 'You guys go out there. Georgie can introduce you to Nick and Amanda.'

As they stepped out of the door, Georgie looked back at Ruth, searching for her reaction.

Ruth smiled and gave her a cheesy thumbs up.

'He seems nice,' Sarah said, opening the fridge.

Ella grinned. 'I'm actually jealous.'

Ruth frowned. 'Too good to be true?' she joked.

'Mum!' Ella sighed.

Sarah shook her head. 'Go and have a cigarette by the bins.'

Ruth laughed. 'Charming!'

Chapter 61

Garrow slumped onto the sofa. It was early evening and he'd made the decision not to go to Ruth's home that afternoon. Instead, he was going to spend the time making sure that his house was tidy and clean. Wash all his clothes for the coming week. He planned to start Monday morning as he meant to go on. Getting control back in his life, which he knew would lessen the free-floating anxiety that he was experiencing.

Even though he still had the whole rigmarole of a police disciplinary to navigate, things still seemed a lot brighter than a few days ago when he was in a drunken state, believing that he had killed Lucy Morgan.

Turning on the television, he was looking forward to watching the BBC's *Antiques Roadshow* which he always found incredibly relaxing. TV Radox is how he liked to describe the programme.

The tail end of the local BBC news was on, and Garrow wondered what the weather was going to be like in the coming week in North Wales.

However, a photograph of a man's face came onto the screen.

Garrow recognised him, but for a moment he couldn't remember how or why.

Then he got a sinking feeling in the pit of his stomach.

Jasper!

The BBC newsreader said, 'North Wales Police are appealing for witnesses after a man's body was found on farmland just outside Wrexham last night. The victim, Jasper Maclean, was found in Ruabon with serious head injuries at around midnight. He died at the scene. Police have launched a murder enquiry and are appealing for anyone who saw anything suspicious in the area at that time to contact them immediately.'

Enjoy this book?
Get the next book in the series
'The Abersoch Killings'

https://www.amazon.co.uk/dp/B0D4MFC6LL

https://www.amazon.com/dp/ B0D4MFC6LL

The Abersoch Killings
A Ruth Hunter Crime Thriller #Book 21

'Last Night At Villa Lucia'

UK https://www.amazon.co.uk/dp/B0CW1KBHTF/

US https://www.amazon.com/dp/B0CW1KBHTF/

THE OPENING CHAPTER TO

'LAST NIGHT AT VILLA LUCIA'

Prologue

I'm sitting in my favourite spot. I lean forward on the wicker sofa with soft plum-coloured cushions, which is carefully positioned in the shade, just to the left-hand side of my villa.

My villa? It still sounds peculiar and rather grandiose. Even after nearly two years. You'd think I'd have got used to it. I guess it's all part of my imposter syndrome. It's my default position for most things.

The sofa has that little creak as I shift my weight. The tightly wound bamboo readjusting.

And though it's not even 8 a.m., the blazing Tuscan sunshine is already blinding and the air temperature oven hot. A fly buzzes past totally oblivious to what's happened this morning. Or maybe it's a sign. An omen.

I gaze out at the view which I've been looking at every morning for two years. The crest of the hill. The expansive vineyard and then beyond that, sprawling fields, a wood and low rolling hills for as far as the eye can see. It's breathtaking. A spectrum of colour. A landscape speckled by a handful of caramel-brown terracotta roofs of distant villas and farmhouses. Over to my right, an olive grove, golden fields and rows of umbrella-shaped trees. To say that it is idyllic doesn't do it justice.

One of the guests at the villa a few months earlier brought paints and sketch books. He told me about the nineteenth-century Italian artist, Giovanni Fattori, a leading figure of the Macchiaioli. Apparently it referred to a group of Tuscan painters whose use of natural light and colour when painting the landscape of the area was highly influential on the French impressionists. I pretended to be fascinated as he waffled on. And his attempts to capture this view – *my view* – were less than impressive. Better than I could do, granted. But then again, I don't paint anymore, nor would I make a big show of landscape painting if the result was on a par with the work of an eight-year-old. I'm being bitchy. My head is throbbing.

However, this morning, I'm unable to take any of this astonishing view in.

My mind is spinning and out of control.

'My view' has taken on a whole new significance today. I've no idea how all this is going to end. But I am starting to realise that this view may not be 'my view' for very much longer.

I take my Chanel sunglasses which have been pushed up into my hair and pop them on the bridge of my nose. I spotted them on a stall in Portobello Market in Notting Hill about six years ago. The stallholder assured me they were vintage. I thought they looked like the kind of sunglasses I'd seen Brigitte Bardot or Sophia Loren wearing in the seventies and parted with the best part of £200. I've had enough compliments to know that they were worth the investment.

I move a strand of my dirty-blonde hair from my face, tuck it behind my ear and notice that my hand is shaking.

It's not surprising after the events of the past half hour. For a moment, I hold my right hand out and watch it quiver. I take a deep breath and try to let it out in a long, slow, controlled stream but the shaking doesn't stop. I need a drink.

By this time of the morning, I would have usually completed my sunrise kundalini yoga class for the guests before making sure that everything is in order for their breakfast. Kiwis, bananas and mangos would have been peeled and chopped. A selection of pastries taken from the freezer to be baked. The coffee machine primed with Melozio pods that are a glorious golden colour. The packet claims they're a harmonious blend of Italian Arabicas with a distinctly sweet note. The split roast adds to the smooth taste and a touch of milk develops a biscuity note.

I'm not sure about any of that. I just know it tastes bloody lovely. I wish that caffeine was my only drug of choice.

And after breakfast is prepared for the guests, I usually wander up to this sofa with my phone, a book and a large glass of cucumber water.

Then it's a ten-minute meditation with a lovely Canadian man called Mike on an app on my phone. He has a comforting, chatty voice that I find very alluring. In fact, until I saw a photo of him, I had imagined him to be a beautiful, dark, handsome man with a beard, in his forties, sitting in white flowing clothes by a lake. Unfortunately, Jeff is in his sixties, with a pointed, weaselly face and glasses. I regret ever looking him up on Google now.

Sometimes, I can find the peace and serenity that I strive for in these guided meditations. Other times, my mind is whirring with anxiety.

And this morning I don't have a glass of cucumber water, a book or my phone.

I'm feeling overwhelmed. Completely overwhelmed by a dread that is making my stomach muscles tighten like a clenched fist. A nasty ball of terror deep inside.

Breathe, Cerys. Just breathe, I tell myself.

So I begin the breathing exercises that I was shown back in those dark days in London. Days when my life was dominated by panic attacks and fear. Before I came to my villa.

In for five, hold for seven, breathe out for eight, I say to myself. *In for five, hold for seven, breathe out for eight.*

It doesn't seem to be working. My pulse is racing.

In for five, hold for seven, breathe out for eight.

I feel like I'm hanging on to my sanity by my fingertips. I close my eyes to steady myself.

In for five, hold for seven, breathe out for eight.

It's no use.

I need to move and not sit still.

I stand up, take a few steps onto the grass and gaze over at the beautiful infinity pool.

I can hardly dare to look – but I force myself.

Oh God.

For a second, I wonder if I had some perverse hallucination when I came out of the villa to lay out guest towels on the sunloungers.

But it's as real as the sun beating down on this terrace.

I go back and sit on the edge of the sofa.

The wind picks up and the air smells of pine.

And then the sound of a police siren fractures the tranquillity.

I wait for them to arrive.

I wonder how this has all happened and how it's all going to end.

Because floating in the middle of my infinity pool, there is a dead body face down in the water.

'Last Night At Villa Lucia'

UK https://www.amazon.co.uk/dp/B0CW1KBHTF/

US https://www.amazon.com/dp/B0CW1KBHTF/

Your FREE book is waiting for you now

Get your FREE copy of the prequel to
the DI Ruth Hunter Series NOW
http://www.simonmccleave.com/vip-email-club
and join my VIP Email Club

DC RUTH HUNTER SERIES

London, 1997. A series of baffling murders. A web of political corruption. DC Ruth Hunter thinks she has the brutal killer in her sights, but there's one problem. He's a Serbian war criminal who died five years earlier and lies buried in Bosnia.

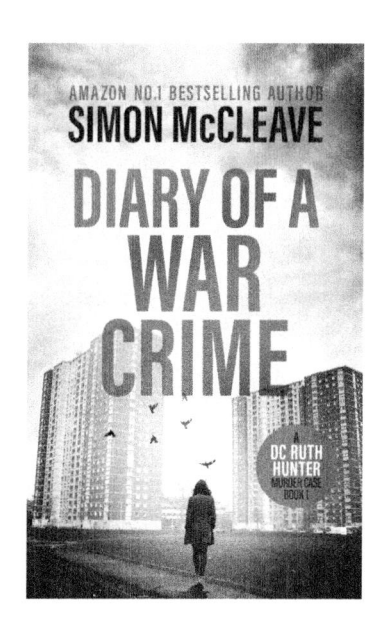

My Book
My Book

AUTHOR'S NOTE

Although this book is very much a work of fiction, it is located in Snowdonia, a spectacular area of North Wales. It is steeped in history and folklore that spans over two thousand years. It is worth mentioning that Llancastell is a fictional town on the eastern edges of Snowdonia. I have made liberal use of artistic licence, names and places have been changed to enhance the pace and substance of the story.

Acknowledgments

I will always be indebted to the people who have made this novel possible.

My mum, Pam, and my stronger half, Nicola, whose initial reaction, ideas and notes on my work I trust implicitly. Carole Kendal for her meticulous proofreading. My designer Stuart Bache for yet another incredible cover design. My superb agent, Millie Hoskins at United Agents, and Dave Gaughran for his invaluable support and advice.